THE DETECTIVE

NORCROSS SECURITY #7

ANNA HACKETT

The Detective

Published by Anna Hackett

Cover by Lana Pecherczyk

Cover image by Wander Aguiar

Edits by Tanya Saari

ISBN (ebook): 978-1-922414-46-5

ISBN (paperback): 978-1-922414-47-2

WHAT READERS ARE SAYING ABOUT ANNA'S ACTION ROMANCE

Heart of Eon - Romantic Book of the Year (Ruby) winner 2020

Cyborg - PRISM Award Winner 2019

Edge of Eon and Mission: Her Protection - Romantic Book of the Year (Ruby) finalists 2019

Unfathomed and Unmapped - Romantic Book of the Year (Ruby) finalists 2018

Unexplored – Romantic Book of the Year (Ruby) Novella Winner 2017

Return to Dark Earth – One of Library Journal's Best E-Original Books for 2015 and two-time SFR Galaxy Awards winner

At Star's End – One of Library Journal's Best E-Original Romances for 2014

The Phoenix Adventures – SFR Galaxy Award Winner for Most Fun New Series and "Why Isn't This a Movie?" Series

Beneath a Trojan Moon – SFR Galaxy Award Winner and RWAus Ella Award Winner

Hell Squad – SFR Galaxy Award for best Post-Apocalypse for Readers who don't like Post-Apocalypse

"Like Indiana Jones meets Star Wars. A treasure hunt with a steamy romance." – SFF Dragon, review of *Among Galactic Ruins*

"Action, danger, aliens, romance – yup, it's another great book from Anna Hackett!" – Book Gannet Reviews, review of *Hell Squad: Marcus*

Sign up for my VIP mailing list and get your *free box set* containing three action-packed romances.

Visit here to get started: www.annahackett.com

CHAPTER ONE

The thump of the music vibrated through the wall.

Detective Hunter Morgan scowled and watched the coffee in his mug ripple in time with the sound waves.

He set the mug down on his coffee table with a sigh. It was late. He'd had a long day at the station, juggling close to a dozen cases. Once he'd gotten home, he'd stripped off his jacket, tie, and holster, and changed into comfortable clothes. All he wanted now was some peace and quiet.

But his new neighbor of the past few weeks wasn't letting that happen.

With a low growl, he stalked out of his living room and down the stairs. He'd bought the three-story townhouse at Hunters Point a year ago. After the U.S. Navy had cleaned up the old Naval shipyard, it had been redeveloped. Now it was filled with new townhouses, amenities, and parks, all with a view of San Francisco Bay.

Hunt loved sitting in his open plan kitchen and living area and watching the ships go by. His top floor bedroom also had a view of the city to the north. Best of all, it was only a ten-minute drive to the Public Safety Building that housed the San Francisco police station where he worked.

Now, his new neighbor was disturbing his sanctuary. She had music thumping at all hours of the night, and through their shared wall, he often heard her making clunking noises as she moved things around.

He'd knocked on her door before, but she'd never answered.

He'd looked into her. Savannah Cole was a graphic designer and was squeaky clean.

Too clean.

Hunt didn't trust clean. His time in the military, and then with the SFPD, had taught him that no one was black or white, good or bad. People were shades of gray, usually shot through with some wild color every now and then.

Anyway, he'd had enough.

He opened his front door. Despite being summer, the night was cool, especially with the breeze coming in off the water. He'd changed into jeans and a T-shirt, and he hadn't even bothered with shoes. He was going to talk to Ms. Cole if he had to ram her door down to get to her.

He crossed to her front door. Their townhouses shared a wall, and like his, the façade of hers was made up of a combination of cream stucco and wood siding. He thumped his fist on the door and waited.

No response.

He thumped again, a little harder, and kept going. He wasn't even sure she could hear him over the music. His anger was on a low simmer. There were families in the complex, kids who'd be sleeping, so her inconsiderate music was affecting more than just him.

He rapped again. If she didn't—

The door opened.

And Hunt found himself staring into a pair of blue eyes so light, they looked gray.

He was six foot three, so she seemed small, but he knew from his background check that she was five foot five.

Her slim body was dwarfed by a huge, white men's shirt, that was currently splattered with paint, and he noticed the hem of tiny, denim shorts peeking from beneath. The shorts showed off her bare legs that ended with toenails painted a bright yellow.

He jerked his gaze back up. The pale-blonde hair had some curl to it, and it was piled on top of her head in a messy knot.

She eyed him with those gray eyes, sharp and filled with annoyance.

"Detective," she said, in a voice that made him think of late-nights and silk sheets. "You planning to hammer a hole in my door?"

"If you'd answered the first time, I wouldn't have had to." He tilted his head. "You know who I am?"

She leaned against the doorjamb. "Detective Hunter Morgan. Oh, the neighborhood loves to gossip over its heroic detective." She swiveled and headed back up the stairs. "If you're coming in, close the door." She disappeared.

Hunt yanked his gaze off her shapely legs and scowled. He closed the door. The place had the same layout as his. The lower floor had a small entry, and the garage off to one side, and a bedroom and bath on the other. Being a detective, he snooped.

The garage was empty, with just a few boxes stacked against the wall. That jived since he hadn't found a car registered in her name. The bedroom was being used for storage. He frowned. It was filled with rolls of what looked like canvas leaning against the wall and lots of boxes.

What the hell?

He stomped up the stairs and the music got louder. The scent of paint hit him. Was she decorating?

He reached the living area and froze.

Savannah stood at a large easel that held a huge canvas. It was partly filled with paint, and she was busy stroking a brush over it. For some reason, the way she held the brush made him think of a female warrior with a sword in hand, about to head into battle.

"Come here," she said, not even looking at him.

Music throbbed from a small speaker. Joan Jett's gritty voice was front and center.

Savannah snatched up a piece of netting off a side table that was covered with an array of unusual items. She pressed it to the canvas.

"Hold that." She grabbed his hand and pressed it to the netting.

Then she started splattering paint again... All over his hand.

Scowling, Hunt watched her face. She was completely absorbed by her work. Then she stepped back, nodded, and smiled.

Hunt's gut knotted. That smile lit up her entire face.

She lifted her gaze and saw him watching her. Her smile vanished. She had a long, narrow face, and high cheekbones.

She set the brush down, grabbed a rag, and wiped her hands. "You did well, Detective." She handed a rag to him, as well.

The music was still thumping, echoing in his ears. He wiped his hands and turned the speaker off. "We haven't been officially introduced."

Her lips quirked. "No, we haven't. But we both know that you already know my name."

"Savannah Cole."

"And now we've met." She headed to her kitchen. It was neat as a pin, and made him think that she didn't cook. She filled a glass with water. As she drank it, he watched the slim line of her throat.

"You're an artist."

Smiling, she set the glass down. "With those keen powers of observation, you must be a very good detective."

Ms. Cole clearly had no problem with sarcasm.

"You sell these?" He glanced around, there were several other finished paintings leaning against the walls. Then he looked back at her. He caught a quick look of grief before she hid it. *Hmm.* His instincts flared to life.

"This is a hobby," she said. "Graphic design is my bread-and-butter."

He studied the wild, passionate painting she was working on. It was of the Bay, the waters looking moody. Or at least, he thought it was. There was a surreal quality to it, like he was looking at it in a dream.

This definitely looked like more than a hobby to him, but what did he know about art?

"You play your music so loud that my walls shake," he said.

She ran her tongue over her teeth. "Sorry. I lose myself when I'm working."

"There are kids in the neighboring homes—"

"I'll keep it down." A strand of hair had escaped the bun, caressing her neck. It looked like spun gold, and he had the oddest urge to touch it.

He eyed her. His gut said that what he saw here was only the tip of the iceberg. He wanted to know more.

"So, where you from?" he asked.

She moved to the sink to wash up the glass, not looking at him. "All around. My family moved around a lot."

That was a well-practiced non-answer. "Where were you born?"

Her head flicked up. "Interrogating me, Detective Morgan?"

Prickly thing. "No. Just being neighborly."

"Right." She moved to the stairs. "I'll see you out."

Ah, he'd been given his marching orders. He followed her down.

"I will try to keep the music down." She opened her

front door. "I don't want to get arrested for disturbing the peace." Her voice was dry.

But as Hunt watched, she scanned the quiet street outside. Her face was alert, watchful.

He straightened. What had Savannah Cole looking so carefully over her shoulder?

Every instinct he had stood up and shouted at him.

"Savannah—"

"It was nice to meet you." She practically shoved him out the door. "Good night, Detective."

She slammed the door shut between them.

Hunt crossed his arms over his chest and stared at the wood. Something was definitely off about his new neighbor.

He was a cop. It was his duty to find out exactly what it was.

And it had *nothing* to do with the long, appealing length of her bare legs.

SAVANNAH COLE SAGGED against the door, closed her eyes, and blew out a breath.

Her new neighbor was hot with a very large H.

As an artist, she appreciated men of all shapes and sizes. She saw the beauty in slim, androgynous, pretty faces, as well as big, fit, streamlined athletes.

But apparently her body had decided tough, slightly scowly, with a rock-solid, muscular body was exactly what lit her fire.

Shaking her head, she started up the stairs. Detective Hunter Morgan was *not* for her.

She could practically see that steel-trap mind of his working overtime. He was a man who'd demand answers, who'd work to uncover every secret.

And Savannah had a truckload of secrets, and no answers to give.

Back in her living room, she stared at the painting she was working on. She was mixing in textures. It was mostly blues, inspired by the shifting waters of the Bay. Sadness cut through her like a blade.

And no one would ever see it.

She had to keep her passion hidden, had to deny her attraction to men like Hunter Morgan.

She didn't get to live a normal life. There was too much at stake.

Dragging in a breath, she waited for the pain to pass. She'd already stayed in San Francisco too long, but she loved the city.

She loved riding her bicycle through the shipyard area. Loved visiting galleries and museums. Loved the artsy vibe of the Mission District.

She'd been here six months. At first, she'd rented a small apartment in the Castro. Then the chance to house-sit this townhouse for a couple currently overseas had turned up. It had been perfect for her.

Savannah knew she should uproot and leave. She should dump the stuff she didn't need, buy a shitty, second-hand car and go. Maybe she'd head south, to Arizona or New Mexico.

Looking at her canvas, her heart clenched. Once

again, she'd have to get rid of all her paintings and sculptures. Once, her art had been celebrated, admired by hundreds.

Now, she had to hide it.

She liked graphic design and doing digital art, but it didn't feed her soul like using a brush, palette knife, or clay did. But doing graphic design meant it was easy to keep her style generic, and she had several online accounts set up across the world. It made it easier to shuffle her money around and avoid detection.

She rubbed her throbbing temple. Life could be so horribly unfair. She thought of her mom and brother, and prayed that they were okay. She thought of her best friend Saskia. She thought of them, missed them, every day.

Maybe she'd head down to LA one day, find a Dark Web hacker, and send her mom an encrypted email.

No. They were safer not knowing where she was.

Anger, grief, and rage welled inside her.

She was the victim of a psychopath, and yet she paid the price over and over again.

Snatching up her palette knife, emotions welled through her. She wanted to turn the music back on, but she didn't need Detective Morgan back at her door. Smelling good—like sandalwood and man—and looking good, tempting her with things she couldn't have.

She ripped open her paints and dipped the knife in. Violent red. *Excellent.*

She attacked a new canvas.

Soon, she was lost in it. Every part of her was engrossed, letting the emotions inside her pour out. She worked hard, desperate to capture the beautiful moment that formed in her head, borne of wants, needs, and desires she had to deny.

She had no idea how long she worked. When she finally stepped back, she was exhausted. Her lower back ached, and she set the palette knife down and stretched.

Then her gaze fell on the canvas and she sucked in a breath.

It was a couple. They were surrounded by flames. It was done in her old, signature style, with blotches of paint giving an impressionist feel. It burst with emotion, passion, and sensuality.

She couldn't do her art like this anymore, because it was too recognizable.

In the painting, the man was dressed, with a hint of a business shirt, tie, and short brown hair. The woman was naked. She was arched back, surrendering to her lover. He held her thigh pressed tight to his hip and his mouth was at her breast. Her blonde hair fell down like a rain of pale gold.

Savannah shifted, feeling desire simmer in her belly. She hadn't been with a man in so long and she'd forgotten what it felt like to have a hard cock slide inside her, filling her up.

She bit her lip and stared at the painting.

Clearly the detective had made an impression.

She opened the door to the small balcony and stepped into the cool night air. Pressing her hands to the railing, she let the air wash over her.

She had to stay away from Hunter Morgan. She had four more months of housesitting. There was no rental agreement, or bills with her name on them. The name she was very aware Morgan suspected was fake.

It was, but it was a good fake. She'd paid a fortune for it.

Susannah Hart was dead. She couldn't go back and paint a target on the people she loved.

She'd protect them the only way she knew how.

That meant running, and being Savannah Cole.

And she'd protect herself, as well. She didn't want to die. She may not get to live the life she'd once dreamed about: a successful art career, a hot, sexy man, and a home with a light-filled studio for her to work in.

But she could steal little moments of life here and there. Then she'd move. Staying on the run was the only way to avoid the very sick man who was obsessed with her.

She lifted her head, and spotted a lone figure at the end of the street. She stiffened. The man was wearing a hoodie, and mostly hidden in the shadows.

Her mouth went dry, and her heart started pounding. For a second, she worried a panic attack was going to hit. She hadn't had one in over a year.

Then the figure turned and walked away, swallowed up by the night.

Savannah released a shaky breath, and squeezed the railing with her fingers. Just someone out for a late-night walk.

When she'd first gone on the run, she'd seen her stalker everywhere. In fact, he'd almost caught her three times.

She released another breath. She'd gotten better at

laying low and running. He'd never touch her, or her family, again.

Savannah slipped back inside and closed the sliding door.

This was just another reminder that there would be no sexy detectives for her.

CHAPTER TWO

Hunt slipped on his shoulder holster, then checked his SIG Sauer and slid the handgun in.

Bright-morning sunshine filled his stylish and well-equipped kitchen. His mom had delighted in helping him pick all the fixtures for his place. He filled a travel mug with coffee—strong and black. He took a sip, his mind running through all the cases he needed to follow up on today.

Out his window, he noticed a bicycle coming down the street. Sunlight glinted off blonde hair.

He stepped closer to the glass.

Savannah slowed, then got off her bike. There was a bunch of fresh flowers in the basket. Today, she was wearing formfitting, black yoga pants, and a slouchy tank top in a pinky-gray color. A shot of male appreciation filled him.

She disappeared from view, and still he stayed there, staring. The last thing he had time for was getting mixed up with his sexy, mysterious artist neighbor.

His cell phone rang. *Shit.* He hoped no one had gotten murdered. His brother's name appeared on the display, and he smiled. "Hi, Cam."

"Hey, Hunt."

Hunt had two brothers. All three of them had joined the military, and Hunt had loved it. He'd found a calling there, and had worked with some of the best, most honorable men and women he'd ever met. Delta Force had pushed him, and he'd gotten to serve his country and make a difference.

Then, a bad parachute landing had blown out his knee. He'd still gotten the mission done, but he'd been told that he couldn't go back to special forces.

It had hurt. Losing something he loved, the chance to make a difference, and failing his team... His hand clenched on his mug. He'd been bitter for a while, before he'd accepted it.

Then, he'd learned that his team had a mission go bad. Even now, his gut tied up in knots. Three men, brothers in arms, hadn't made it back. Two of them had been married with kids, the third had a pregnant fiancée.

He hadn't been there for them.

"Hunt?" Cam's gritty voice came through the line.

His brother had recently gotten out of Ghost Ops. A special, covert team made up of the best of the best across special forces. They did the hardest, toughest missions. Their middle brother, Ryder, had been out a few years. He'd been a combat medic in the Air Force.

Ryder was now a part-time paramedic, and worked at a free clinic in the Tenderloin. Camden had taken a job in private security. He now worked for Hunt's friend, Vander Norcross, at Norcross Security.

"Sorry," Hunt said. "How's it going, Cam?"

"Fine."

There was something buried deep in Cam's voice. He wasn't fine. Not yet.

"Settling in at Norcross?" Hunt asked.

"It's only my second day. Vander runs a tight ship."

Hunt really wanted to know how Cam was doing. He'd had a bomb explode on his team. His physical scars were healing, but he'd lost people.

A person never really got over that. Hunt was pretty sure that Camden wasn't ready to talk, but Hunt would be there for him, any way he needed him.

"I was calling to see if you wanted to catch up tonight?" Cam said. "Grab some dinner."

"Sure. Beer and burger at Harry's?" The sports bar was one of their favorites.

"Sounds good. I'll see if Ryder's free, too. See you then."

"Great. Bye, Cam."

Hunt stared out the window at the Bay, not really seeing the gleaming water. Cam needed time, and Hunt knew that better than anyone.

On the plus side, Vander would keep an eye on him. Vander was former Ghost Ops as well. Norcross Security would give Cam a sense of purpose, just as the police force had done for Hunt. He'd found his new calling as a cop.

He grabbed his car keys and headed downstairs. He drove an unmarked Dodge Charger. He'd gotten in late the day before, so he'd parked on the street out front, rather than in his garage.

His downstairs bedroom was set up as a gym. He'd already worked out this morning, and hit his rowing machine hard. He swam a couple of times a week as well, when he could fit it in. Once, he'd loved to run, but his messed-up knee ruled that out these days.

He locked his front door, juggling his travel mug and his suit jacket that he'd slung over his arm, just as Savannah came out of her front door.

They eyed each other warily.

"Morning," he said.

"Good morning." Her gaze dropped to his holster. "You look very...detective-like today."

His lips twitched. "And you look very artist-like."

She raised a brow.

"You have paint on your cheek." He pulled a clean handkerchief from his pocket and wiped the mark.

This close to her, she smelled like paint and flowers. It seemed like the perfect combination for her.

She was still, those big gray eyes watching him steadily.

"Detective Morgan," a singsong female voice called out.

Savannah stepped back, her gaze unsettled.

"Don't go," he said quietly. There might have been a touch of panic to his tone.

Now amusement sparked in the gray. "Surely you aren't afraid of one overly friendly woman?"

"Savannah—"

"Good morning!" Denise Morford stopped in front of

them, a huge smile on her face. She was an attractive forty-something, twice divorced, and on the hunt for husband number three. She wore a snug skirt that hugged her hips, a white tank with a deep *V* to show off her impressive cleavage, and lots of statement necklaces made of colorful stones. She designed jewelry and sold it online for a living.

"Morning, Denise," he said.

"Hunt, you're looking tired today." Denise smiled. "You should let me make you a nice, home-cooked meal tonight."

"Sorry, I can't. I have plans already."

"I'll leave you guys to it." With an amused smile, Savannah crossed the street. He watched her go, heading over to where Mrs. Romero was watering the pots of flowers she kept out in front of her place.

"So, maybe another night then?" Denise asked hopefully.

Hunt watched Savannah talk with Mrs. Romero. The older widow beamed at Savannah and pinched her cheek.

There was no prickliness in sight from his neighbor.

"Hunt?"

He blinked and looked back at Denise. "I can't, Denise. Sorry. Work's really busy."

Her face fell. "Of course. You work so hard."

He looked up and saw Savannah hand something to Mrs. Romero. The old woman looked thrilled.

He squinted and realized it was a small painting...of the older lady's pots of flowers. It was done in an abstract style, bursting with color.

"Well, then..." Denise tucked her brown hair behind her ear. "I'll just—"

Hunt's phone rang. Vander's name came up on the screen. "I need to take this. Excuse me." He pressed it to his ear. "Vander."

"Hey, Hunt." The deep voice of Vander Norcross came across the line.

"You'd better still be making my cousin a happy woman." When Hunt noted Denise listening intently, he smiled, and stepped back inside his townhouse to avoid the nosiness.

Two months back, Vander—a dangerous man with a scary reputation in San Francisco—had helped out Hunt's cousin, Detective Brynn Sullivan.

During their time in the military, Vander and Hunt had worked together a few times, until Vander had been recruited to run a shadowy Ghost Ops team.

Now, Hunt was usually left cleaning up the mess Vander and his team at Norcross left whenever they tackled a job in the city. He'd intervened more times than he could count to deal with high-speed chases, beaten-up bad guys, and dead bodies. He didn't always agree with Vander's tactics—which included doing whatever the hell he thought was necessary and damn the rules—but Hunt knew Vander was a good man.

Shockingly, Vander had taken the ultimate fall, and fallen in love with Brynn. The pair were crazy about each other. Brynn was now happily living in Vander's loft above the Norcross Security warehouse.

"Well, she was a happy woman this morning." Vander's tone held a touch of smugness.

Hunt groaned. "No details. *Please.*"

He didn't need to imagine Vander and Brynn that way. Hunt was damn glad that Brynn was happy, and while Vander hadn't softened much, he seemed a little less intense.

"I wanted to discuss a case with you," Vander said.

"Sure. And I wanted to ask about Cam."

Vander sighed. "He needs time, Hunt, but he'll get there. We all did. We can help smooth the way for him."

"Thanks, Vander. Now tell me about your case."

"THANK YOU, LOVELY GIRL."

Savannah smiled at sweet Mrs. Romero.

The woman loved her flowers, loved to talk, and often dropped off a loaf of freshly made bread for Savannah.

"I'm glad you like it." It had only taken her minutes to put together the little painting of Mrs. Romero's flowers.

"I sent a picture of the last one you did to my son and daughter-in-law. They live in New York. So far away. But they loved seeing your beautiful painting."

The mention of New York sent a pang through Savannah. She'd never, ever go home again.

She turned her head and watched a dejected Denise walking away. Detective Morgan stood with the phone pressed to his ear, unlocking his front door.

How could the man look so hot just talking on the phone? And the shoulder holster didn't help. He looked scrumptious.

Her fingers itched to sketch him. He disappeared

back inside. Denise, her romantic intentions thwarted, headed back down the street to her place. She seemed like a nice lady. Savannah couldn't blame the woman for trying.

"I'll make you some more sourdough." Mrs. Romero patted Savannah's arm. "I know how much you like it."

She smiled. "Thanks, Mrs. R."

But inside, Savannah felt a niggle. Mrs. R knew that Savannah liked bread. Ella-Mae, who lived three doors down, was in high school, and loved to pepper Savannah with art questions. The girl was a budding artist who liked to paint. And then there was the nosy detective who was just a little too curious.

Yeah, she'd been here too long.

Suddenly, loud shouts down the street made her stiffen.

Mrs. R's face paled. "Oh, no."

Savannah pivoted, and her gut knotted.

A man stormed out of one of the townhouses, arms waving, body language aggressive. His wife stepped out behind him, holding her thin body stiffly. When he yelled again, the woman flinched.

John Garoppolo bellowed some more, and Marcie flinched again. Her blonde hair was lank and loose.

"You were flirting with him," John roared.

"I just said hello to—"

"Shut up, you whore."

Enough. "Excuse me, Mrs. Romero."

"Savannah, maybe—"

"It'll be fine." Savannah strode toward the fighting couple. As she got closer, her jaw tightened.

Marcie had a black eye.

"John," Savannah said. "Marcie."

The man whirled. He wasn't tall, but he was stocky, with a swarthy face and some Italian heritage. He'd probably been handsome once.

In high school, he'd probably been the good-looking athlete who the girls flocked to. He probably thought he'd be rich and successful one day.

Instead, he was a mediocre shmoe who worked some desk job, had put on a few pounds, and whose hair had thinned.

As she got closer, she smelled stale alcohol. He'd clearly had a big night.

"Why don't you head back inside, John? Marcie, would you like to come to my place to have a cup of tea?"

"Shut up, bitch," John spat.

Marcie flinched, but Savannah just crossed her arms. She'd heard worse. Way worse.

"Look, Marcie and I will just—"

"You'll do *nothing*." John's face scrunched. "Marcie is my useless, cheating wife. She stays with me."

Savannah straightened. The guy was a bully. She hated bullies.

And she was no one's damn victim.

"She doesn't belong to you, asshole."

Marcie gasped. "Savannah, please don't..." Her face was pinched with fear.

She was so terrified. She'd probably married the guy with stars in her eyes, thinking she'd found her prince charming. Until her prince and dream had all gone sour.

Why was it that the worst monsters looked normal? Savannah knew that better than anyone.

"Come with me, Marcie." She held out a hand.

"She's not going anywhere with you," John roared. He grabbed the front of Marcie's shirt.

The woman sucked in a breath, then he shoved her against the side of the house.

"Hey!" Savannah yelled.

She saw others on the street, watching restlessly, looking upset. She spotted Ella-Mae. The teenager's face was sheet-white. As John slammed Marcie again, the woman cried out in pain.

Anger ignited in Savannah. She caught Ella-Mae's gaze. "Get Hunter. Go."

With a nod, the teen took off down the street.

Savannah grabbed a handful of the back of John's T-shirt.

"Let her go," Savannah said. "*Now.*"

With a grunt, he spun. "You should have stayed out of our business."

"You bullying and roughing up your wife, or any woman, is everyone's business."

His hands flexed. "You're just another whore."

"You're just another asshole."

With an ugly growl, he stepped into her space. Savannah felt a shot of fear, absorbed it. She knew the source of it was old. One that she would never let define her.

She lifted her chin. "What are you going to do, John? The whole street is watching."

He glanced around, clearly noting their worried neighbors.

She jerked her head to the side. "Come on, Marcie." Savannah couldn't stop a faint smile. There was nothing better than assholes getting beaten.

Marcie looked frozen; her hand fluttered toward Savannah before she pressed it to her neck, instead. She looked so uncertain and afraid.

Then the woman took a step toward her, and John snapped.

"No! The bitch is mine. You fucking stay out of this." He swung his arm and caught Savannah in the face.

His fist wasn't quite closed—it was a half punch, half slap. He hit her jaw and mouth. Pain exploded, and she tasted blood.

And her anger.

No asshole would hit her, hurt her, or scar her again.

She heard shouts, but her vision formed a tunnel. Fueled by her rage, she launched at John. He wasn't expecting it.

She tackled him to the ground, with her landing on top. His head hit the concrete and he bellowed.

"You don't get to hurt people, asshole." She gripped his shirt. "You—"

He swung at her again.

His fist never connected.

Savannah was suddenly pulled backward. Her back hit a hard wall of chest and she turned her head, and looked into the coldly furious eyes of Hunter Morgan.

That green gaze swept over her, pausing on her

mouth. She felt his anger swelling. Something flashed in the green, and his jaw tightened.

He set her down, then turned. He towered over John who was still sprawled on the sidewalk.

"Arrest her, Hunt," the man spluttered. "She attacked me. I was just—"

Hunt leaned down and dragged the man up. "You don't want to say anything, Garoppolo."

The lethal tone made goose bumps erupt on Savannah's arms. Man, she never, ever wanted Hunter Morgan to use that tone on her.

Hunt hauled John around, and pulled handcuffs off his belt.

"Regina and Ella-Mae, take Marcie inside. Get her a drink and an ice pack."

The teenager and her mother nodded, then ushered the shell-shocked Marcie inside.

Hunt speared Savannah with a laser-sharp gaze. "You, don't move." Then he shoved John face first against the door, and yanked the man's wrists behind his back. "And you be quiet while I read you your rights. You're under arrest."

CHAPTER THREE

Hunt kept a tight grip on his temper as he jerked the handcuffed John around.

A police cruiser turned onto the street. Hunt had called it in. A male and female officer got out. Hunt recognized the woman, a veteran in the SFPD. He handed over the now-silent but still belligerent John.

"Guy hit his wife," Hunt said.

The female officer, Maureen Polansky, glared. The other officer shook his head.

Yeah, they'd seen it all before, but for Hunt, there was a special place in hell for a man who'd hurt someone physically smaller than them—especially a woman or a child. And especially someone you were supposed to love.

"There were lots of witnesses. And he assaulted another woman."

The upside of that was if Marcie decided not to press charges, they could still charge him with hitting Savannah.

Hunt glanced over at Savannah, and rage stirred in his gut. Her lip was swollen and split, and there was dried blood on the corner of her mouth. She leaned against the low, stone wall marking the boundary of the property, watching John with undisguised hatred.

She'd attacked John like she was a tiger, not fifty pounds smaller than the guy.

They'd have a discussion about that later.

"Will the wife press charges?" Polansky asked.

"Not sure. Try your best."

"We've got it from here, Detective," the other officer said.

Hunt turned to Savannah. She watched him coming, those gray eyes full of secrets and wariness.

He gently gripped her chin, studied her lip, and tried to ignore the fact that he also noticed they were perfectly shaped.

She didn't fidget or fuss, and his chest tightened. That told him she'd likely been hit in the face before.

That, he really didn't like.

"Come on." He took her arm and tugged her to her feet. He pulled her toward his place.

"Don't you have to get to work?" she asked.

"I will."

"Surely crime waits for no man."

He unlocked his front door and towed her upstairs. As they entered his living area, she looked around with interest.

"Wow... You're so neat. And *tidy*."

His lips quirked. "You say that like it's a flaw."

He didn't have much in the way of decoration, but

everything *was* neat and tidy. He attributed that to his military training. He did have a nice, framed photo of the San Francisco skyline on the wall.

She made a sound.

Hunt's lips twitched. "We can't all be wild, disorganized artists."

"I'm not disorganized. I know *exactly* where all my stuff is."

"That's impossible." He pulled her into the kitchen, then gripped her slim waist and set her on the island.

She gasped.

And Hunt marveled at the fact that his hands almost spanned her small waist.

He reached over and opened the freezer, pulled out an ice pack, and wrapped it in a kitchen towel. Then he pressed it to her lip.

Savannah pulled in a sharp breath. "I have ice at my place."

"My ice is better." He met her gaze and leaned a hip against the island. "You have a problem letting someone help you?"

She shifted her shoulders, looking uncomfortable. "I'm just used to looking after myself."

Maybe she had to, because she was never anywhere long enough to let anyone close. He noted in his check on Savannah Cole that she didn't have a permanent place of residence.

She waved the ice pack around. "Don't look at me like that."

"Like what?"

"Like I'm a mystery that needs solving."

He pushed the ice pack back on her lip. "If the shoe fits."

"I'm *not* a mystery. I'm a simple woman."

He snorted.

Her eyes narrowed. "I am."

"Sure."

"Sarcasm doesn't become you, Detective Morgan."

"Call me Hunt."

"I like Hunter better." Then she clamped her mouth shut like she hadn't meant to say that.

No one called him Hunter. Even his mom called him Hunt. But he liked the idea of this mysterious, gray-eyed blonde calling him Hunter.

"You can call me Hunter." He cocked his head. "You shouldn't have engaged John."

Her face hardened. "He was hurting Marcie. I wasn't going to let that asshole lay his hands on her again."

The vehemence in her voice made him even more intrigued. "You could've been really hurt."

She shrugged, waving the ice pack around again. "There were people around. I'm not stupid. And I told Ella-Mae to get you right away." She paused. "I had to do something."

He pushed the ice pack back on again.

"The lip is all right," she said. "It'll heal up fast."

"You know this from experience?"

Her gaze shifted, and she suddenly seemed very interested in his backsplash tiles.

"Do you think Marcie will press charges?" she asked.

Hunt sighed. "I've spoken with her before... DV situations are difficult."

"He's a violent, aggressive asshole, so it seems pretty cut and dry to me."

Hunt scraped a hand over his hair. "It should be." But it never was. "Will you press charges?"

Her gaze dropped. "I'm not really hurt..."

"It'll help."

"No." She shook her head.

"Savannah—"

"I can't. I..." She bit her lip.

"Well, let's see how it goes with Marcie, or the asshole will get off."

Savannah's gaze moved back to his face. "I am sorry. You must see assholes get away with all kinds of stuff."

"Yeah." It was the hardest part of his job.

"It sucks that sometimes the bad guys are clever enough to avoid consequences." There was resignation buried deep in her voice. "Life is never fair."

"Hey." Hunt put a finger under her chin. "Life isn't always fair, but it isn't all bad."

She didn't respond, but her fingers circled his wrist. She pushed his hand away, but her gaze locked on it. She got a focused look.

"I want to sculpt your hands."

Hunt frowned. "What?"

"Your hands." She turned his hand over. "They're so strong, and you have long fingers." She stroked her fingers over his knuckles and the scars there. "You have strength. You've lived. Worked. It shows."

"Savannah..."

Her gaze flicked up.

"You'd better stop stroking my hands like that,

because it's giving me ideas, and I have to get to the station."

She dropped his hand like it was on fire. "I need to go." She leaped off the island and dumped the ice pack in the sink. "Um, thanks for the ice, and the help."

"Try not to take on any more abusive assholes today."

That got him a faint smile. "The day is young, so I can't make any promises."

"Keep an eye on that lip."

"Right." She headed for the stairs.

"And Savannah?"

She paused and looked back at him.

"I'm a detective. My job is to solve puzzles. And it's too late, because I'm planning to solve yours."

Her eyes widened, and he caught a flash of strong emotion. Fear, but something else, as well. "Hunter—"

"I'll see you later."

She stared at him for a beat, then fled.

Oh yes, she was definitely a mystery he planned to solve.

SAVANNAH HUNCHED OVER THE TABLE, moving her hands over the clay.

It was coming to life. Matching the picture in her head exactly.

She'd been working feverishly, and lost track of time.

After the drama of the morning, she'd worked at her computer for a bit, and then had finally given in to the urgent, growing need to sketch.

To sketch Hunter.

She'd finally made herself stop, and paint. But those hands—those strong, steady, scarred hands—wouldn't leave her alone. She'd *had* to capture them.

And not with charcoal or paint.

She'd pulled out some clay and gotten to work.

His strong hands were coming to life for her.

She'd captured the strength of the man who stood for others. Who protected. Her sculpture had morphed a little. In it, those strong hands were cradling a set of smaller, more feminine ones between them. She hadn't used her own hands as the template on purpose. It was just the easiest option.

She stroked the clay. *Dammit.* She couldn't hold everything in place in order to get it just right. And she didn't want to use a vise.

A thumping sound interrupted her thoughts.

She frowned.

The thumping came again. She realized someone was hammering on her door.

With an irritated huff, she carefully set the sculpture down and headed down the stairs. She swiped her hands on her shirt.

She yanked open the door. "What?"

Hunter stood on her doorstep. He was still in the suit pants and blue shirt from this morning, but his tie and holster were gone.

"I'm checking on you," he said. "I saw your light on."

She frowned.

"It's midnight," he added.

"It is?" Then she shook her head. "Come here." She grabbed his shirt and yanked him inside.

She realized that her hands were still mostly covered in clay, which was now smeared on his shirt.

But she didn't care about that right now. Her mind was whirling too much to be sorry she'd messed up his shirt. She needed to finish her sculpture.

"Savannah—"

"Shush. Just hurry up." She bounded up the stairs.

She moved back to the plastic-covered dining table. She worked the clay again. She felt almost delirious. She *had* to finish it.

"Here." She grabbed his hands—the real ones. Those big, strong hands that had inspired her. "Hold here. Don't press too hard, or I'll have to kill you."

He made a sound. "I'm a detective, remember? You'd get caught."

"I'd be justified, if you ruin this."

She shifted, her body brushing his. Now that he was holding it, she could work on crafting the female hands clasped gently, but possessively, by those larger male ones.

She lost track of time again, following the vision in her head.

Then finally, it was done.

Savannah straightened, and felt how stiff her back and neck were.

"Can I let go?"

She blinked, Hunt's deep voice bringing her fully back to reality. "Yes."

He stared at the sculpture of the hands. "It's incredible, Savannah. So lifelike."

Did he recognize his own hands? She cleared her throat, and grinned. "It's gorgeous. Just like I pictured it."

He cocked his head. "Is that how it works? You have a picture in your head?"

She nodded. "Like a vision. But usually, I find nothing ever works out quite how you imagine it. That's the struggle of an artist, having this vision, but not having the skills to realize it as perfectly as you want. But this one worked out."

"Does it have a name?"

She met his gaze. "*Strength*. Ah, thanks for the help."

"You didn't give me much choice."

Her smile widened. "And it looks like I owe you a shirt."

He glanced down at the smears and grunted.

Savannah took a step, then swayed.

"Hey." Strong arms slid around her.

"I'm fine. Just lightheaded." The room spun a little.

He guided her to the couch. "When was the last time you ate?"

She wrinkled her nose. "Um, I'm not sure."

"Did you eat dinner?"

"Um..."

"Lunch?" he asked more forcefully.

"Maybe?" She sagged against the cushions. She was pretty sure she'd grabbed a piece of bread and honey at some stage.

Hunt made an unhappy sound and strode to her kitchen. She noted that he always strode, like a man on a mission, a man with a purpose. No lazy stroll for Hunter Morgan.

He washed his hands, then opened her refrigerator. "You know you have one wilted tomato, some juice, butter, and a hunk of cheese?"

"Yep."

He glanced her way. "That's it."

"What are you? The refrigerator police? I need to get some groceries. I have some bread from Mrs. Romero."

Hunt brought her back a glass of water, and a healthy slice of sourdough slathered with butter. He also had a wet cloth.

He sat on the ottoman in front of her, and grabbed her hands. He then set about wiping the clay off them.

Unwelcome heat pooled in her belly. When was the last time someone had taken care of her like this?

Needing a distraction, she snatched up the bread and devoured it. "You're a bit of a mother hen."

A line formed on his brow. "Making sure you don't collapse is just being nice."

"Uh huh." She licked her fingers.

His gaze dropped to her mouth.

A flicker of heat danced in Savannah's belly. Okay, more than a flicker, but less than a raging inferno.

But she knew herself well enough, even if it had been a tragically long time since she'd been with a man, that this thing could grow into raging-inferno territory in a heartbeat, if she let it.

"I had to get the art done. It's a compulsion. When I'm like that, I don't eat, sleep... I just work."

He turned his head to look at the sculpture. "It is impressive. I never considered my hands as artwork."

Ah, so he had recognized them. She fought back the heat filling her cheeks. "I felt inspired. Thanks for the help. I was frustrated that I couldn't get it finished. What time is it?"

"Nearly one in the morning."

"Shit. Well, at least I didn't stay up all night." She eyed him. "You just got home from work?"

"No."

Her stomach did a funny circle. "Date?"

"Dinner with my brothers."

"Oh. Are they cops like you?" She instantly thought of her brother, Ezra, and missed him dreadfully. He'd been a smart-ass, funny, and so much fun. Her heart clenched.

"No. Ryder is a paramedic, and Camden just got out of the military. He's working in private security."

"A family of protectors." Her gaze moved back to the sculpture. God, it was so good. She leaped up. "Look at this. It's so gorgeous."

He came up behind her. "I know nothing about art, but it's amazing, Savannah. You're very talented."

Giddy, she spun, grabbed the collar of his shirt and kissed him.

He froze.

She was feeling too good to process the consequences, and pulled back, smiling. "Thanks again for the help, Detective."

"Wait." His hands clamped on her waist. Then he yanked her forward.

She registered a hard body, but then all she could think about was the firm, mobile mouth capturing hers.

And the deep, slightly bossy kiss he laid on her.

She clung to him, tasting him, her head spinning.

He lifted his head.

"Right. You'd better go. I need sleep." She eyed the clay on his shirt. There was even more now. "Oops, I made it worse. I really owe you a shirt."

"It's fine."

An image of Hunt, with no shirt, lodged in her head. He'd have a tough, muscular body, she could tell. Her throat went dry.

She had to get him out of there before she did something stupid.

Then she grabbed his hand, and towed him down the stairs.

Yes, she needed him gone, before she made a mistake of epic proportions.

He stayed quiet on the journey to her front door.

She yanked the door open. "Good night, Detective."

"Simple woman, my ass." He ran his thumb over her lip, gently moving over where it was cut. "Good night, Savannah."

CHAPTER FOUR

The next morning, Hunt headed out to his Charger. There was no sign of movement at Savannah's. He scowled. She was probably sleeping like a baby. Meanwhile, he felt tired and churned up.

That kiss...

She'd vibrated with passion, then shoved him out the door like he had an infectious disease. He knew she was wary, but still. After helping her with her artwork, he'd thought they'd made a connection. Hell, he'd never felt that feeling before, having a hand in creating something so beautiful.

Sure, putting criminals behind bars gave him a sense of satisfaction, but that was different. That always felt like the end of something bad. But making art felt like the beginning of something good.

And how Savannah had looked after that kiss, her face flushed with desire...

If she poured that much passion into her art, would she give the same level of it in bed? His cock tightened.

Hunt swallowed a groan. He'd dreamed of her. All night. He'd woken with a throbbing cock that he had to take care of in the shower.

Today, he was stopping at the local coffee shop for something with an extra shot before he headed to his desk. He found a parking space and headed inside the Roasted Bean, known to the locals as the Bean.

They were doing a brisk business.

"Hey there, Detective." The pretty brunette at the counter gave him a flirtatious smile. "The usual?"

"Yes, thanks, Sam."

He paid and moved aside, going through his cases in his head. He needed to catch up with Brynn about some gang crime, then follow up with some informants.

Out of the corner of his eye, he saw a bicycle pass by the front window. His muscles tightened, and a moment later, Savannah bustled into the coffeeshop.

She wore another pair of those tiny denim shorts, and a slouchy, white T-shirt. It fell off one shoulder, revealing smooth, golden skin. Her blonde hair was in a ponytail today, and it made her look younger. She headed straight for the counter.

"Vanilla latte. Stat." She smiled, then turned and spotted him. Her smile wavered and she hesitated, then she moved toward him. "Hey."

"Good morning." Damn, just looking at her tied him in knots. He wanted her. Badly. He wasn't a man used to having trouble controlling himself. "How's the lip?"

His gaze went to her pink lips, covered in something glossy. The small injury looked better already.

"Totally fine." Her finger brushed her bottom lip, sending his brain into X-rated territory.

Shit. He put a stranglehold on his out-of-control desire. "Sleep well?"

"Like a baby."

"That makes one of us."

She raised a brow at his grumpy tone. "Rough night?"

He leaned closer. "My sexy neighbor kept me up."

Heat hit her cheeks. "It wasn't that late."

"It wasn't helping you with your art that kept me up." Her hair smelled like fruity shampoo, but still with an undertone of paint that he shouldn't find so alluring. "It was afterward, lying in my bed, hard for you."

Her lips parted. "Hunter..."

"Hi, Savannah. Hi, Detective Morgan."

Hunt made himself step back. Ella-Mae was beaming at them. The teenager was tall and thin, her blonde-brown hair in a braid.

"Hi, Ella-Mae." Savannah shot the girl a bright smile.

"I wanted to ask how Marcie was?" The girl's face filled with worry.

"She's staying with her sister, and sorting out her options." Hunt hoped she picked one where she divorced her abusive husband, but Hunt had heard the excuses she'd made for John—that he was stressed at work, not sleeping well, had some health issues.

It was fifty-fifty as to how it would go for Marcie.

"So, she's safe." Ella-Mae released a breath. "Savannah, you were like Wonder Woman yesterday, diving in there to stop John."

It looked like Ella-Mae had a girl crush.

"She was foolish," Hunt said.

Both women looked at him.

"She could have gotten hurt badly, worse than a split lip."

Savannah straightened. "Morgan—"

He touched a loose strand of her hair and tucked it back behind her ear. "Foolish, but brave."

Some of the fire went out of her eyes.

Hunt noted Ella-Mae looking between the two of them, and her smile—impossibly—got bigger.

"Morgan and Cole," the barista called out.

Ella-Mae nodded. "I'll let you two get back to your coffee date. I need to go."

"It's not a date," Savannah said quickly.

The teenager winked. "Right. Well, I need a chai and a doughnut."

"Shouldn't you be at your summer job?" Savannah asked.

"I have a day off. Bye."

Savannah snatched up her coffee. Hunt reached past her for his own.

"Great, now she thinks we're together," Savannah muttered.

"You have a problem with that?"

"We *aren't* together." She sipped her coffee.

"Yet," he countered.

Her eyes went wide. "What?"

"I like the look of you, Savannah."

She stiffened. "I won't be around long. I don't do relationships."

"You mean you have secrets, and you don't trust

easily."

She looked away and sipped her coffee again.

Hunt moved closer. "I like how you smell like paint. I like the way you look at me, even when you're trying not to. I admire that you rushed in to protect Marcie, even though it was risky. And I like that you really liked my hands. I'm keen to let you study them in more detail."

Those gray eyes met his, boiling with emotion. "Don't do this," she whispered.

"What?"

"Tempt me with things I can't have."

There was so much pain in her voice. He fought back a frown, and the urge to bombard her with questions. A part of him wanted to know who'd hurt her so he could make it go away. It was just how he was built.

Suddenly, he heard the screech of tires outside, and then the distinct sound of gunfire.

The front windows of the Bean shattered.

Hunt acted on instinct. He leaped on Savannah, taking her to the ground.

Screams exploded through the coffee shop, and furniture rattled and shook as patrons dove for cover.

"*Hunt*," she said shakily.

"Stay still," he growled. "Everyone down!"

There was another spray of bullets, and he felt Savannah jolt and press into him. He made sure he kept her covered with his body.

Bullets peppered the counter, pinged off metal and glass. Something broke with a loud crash. Savannah cried out, and he held her tighter.

He'd keep her safe. He hadn't been there for his team in Afghanistan, but he'd be there for Savannah.

Finally, there were no more bullets. There was another screech of tires.

Cautiously, he lifted his head. Sobs and cries filled the coffee shop.

"Hunter." Savannah's fingers curled into his arms.

He kissed her nose. "It's going to be okay."

A teenage boy half rose from behind a chair. "They're gone. The car sped off."

Hunt nodded. "Stay down." He needed to call it in. "Is anyone hurt?"

"My dad's bleeding!" a girl yelled. "Help!"

Shit.

SAVANNAH COULDN'T STOP SHAKING. She dragged in some deep breaths, reminding herself over and over that the danger was gone.

Hunt moved into a crouch and pulled a dangerous-looking handgun out. She watched him scanning the street through the shattered windows.

Savannah jumped up. A middle-aged man was sitting against the wall, a hand pressed to his shoulder. Blood was oozing through his fingers.

She moved to the counter. The baristas were huddled on the floor behind it, terrified.

"It's going to be okay." She grabbed some towels and then moved toward the man. "I'm going to put this on your wound to stop the bleeding."

The man nodded. His daughter seemed to be about ten, and was clinging to his arm. She had a face full of freckles, and looked so pale and scared.

Savannah steeled herself and looked at the man's shoulder. Her stomach rolled a little. "Now, I'm no expert, but it looks like the bullet clipped the top of your shoulder. You should be fine." She pressed the towel harder and hoped to hell she wasn't lying.

Beside the man, the girl whimpered.

Hunt was striding through the store, calming people. Savannah saw the way people watched and listened to him. His authoritative, calm voice soothed them.

It soothed her jittering nerves a little, too.

"Something like this shouldn't happen here," the man said, voice shaky. "It's a safe area. Olivia and I come here multiple times a week. It's our thing. Dad and daughter coffee."

"The police will sort it out."

"I'm scared." Olivia grabbed her dad's hand.

"See that man?" Savannah nodded toward Hunt. "He's a police detective. He catches bad guys."

"He'll catch the shooter?" Olivia brightened a little.

"He'll do everything he can." Savannah shot the girl a confident smile. Crap, she hoped it looked confident.

Moments later, several police cruisers screamed to a halt outside.

Hunt sent her one long glance, then strode out to meet the officers. She looked around. People were coming out of hiding. Some were pointing at the bullet holes, others hugging each other.

She studied the damage. The bullet holes were all clustered around the center of the store.

The hairs on the back of her neck rose.

No.

She swallowed. They were all grouped around where she and Hunt had been standing.

Her heart pounded.

It was just a coincidence. She swallowed again. Her stalker had never shot at her, or used a gun.

That she knew of.

The paramedics arrived next. Hunt pointed toward the man Savannah was helping.

The men, wearing navy-blue uniforms, headed over. One paramedic looked older—probably in his late fifties, head shaved, a graying goatee on his chin. The other one... Wow. He was tall, broad-shouldered, with lean hips. He had longish, brown hair pulled back in a stubby tail, and stubble that suited him mighty fine.

His lips were tipped in a faint smile that promised sin. And his green eyes were the exact same shade as Hunt's.

Her gaze flicked between the two men. They looked similar, except one looked like a clean-cut, handsome, bossy cop, and the other a bad boy, who mothers warned their daughters to avoid.

"Please, step back, ma'am," the older paramedic said. "We'll take it from here."

Savannah rose. She looked up at the hot Morgan paramedic. The man eyed her, his smile widening.

Then Hunter stepped up beside her and slid an arm around her waist. "Dibs."

The paramedic's lips twitched.

Savannah cocked her head. "Did you just call dibs on me?"

"Yes. I have two brothers. I've learned to stake my claim to what I want fast—the last steak, the leftovers, the front seat, whatever."

"Did you just compare me to a steak?"

"I would never do that, beautiful," the paramedic said. "I have way more class than that."

"Your brother's pretty smooth, Hunter," she said.

Hot paramedic winked.

"And cocky," she added.

"He was born that way. Savannah, my brother, Ryder. Ryder, my neighbor, Savannah."

"Ah, now I know why my brother's been grumpy about his new neighbor," Ryder drawled.

She wrinkled her nose. "I've been playing my music too loudly."

Ryder's lips twitched. "Beautiful, that is *not* his problem with you."

Hmm, these Morgan men sure packed a punch. "And there's a third one of you, right?"

"Camden," Hunt said.

Ryder crouched to help his partner, teasing a smile from Olivia.

Hunt got called over by the cops.

Savannah wrapped her arms around her middle, thinking about the bullet holes again. This couldn't be about her. Her mouth was dry, her chest tight. She hated the growing dread inside her.

She'd learned to trust her instincts. They'd kept her alive for too long.

She saw a female cop—a detective by the looks of her—stride into the coffee shop and take everything in with one swift glance. Savannah admired the woman's dark pants and fitted white shirt. She had a badge and a gun on her belt. Her hair—a pretty combination of multiple shades of brown—was in a ponytail.

The woman hurried over to Hunt, then hugged him.

A funny sensation wound through Savannah. They looked good together, dammit. Hunt wasn't hers. She shouldn't feel like this.

Then another man entered the Bean.

Savannah stilled, and fought the urge to duck behind the counter. It wasn't that he was unattractive. He totally was. He had dark good looks and dark hair, and his suit didn't hide his muscular build.

It was that he looked dangerous. He had a vibe that told her that the man could kill everyone in the room without breaking a sweat.

She wanted to paint his face. She'd do it so he was half in shadow, and try and capture his dangerous intensity.

His gaze swept over the room and met hers, held.

Savannah looked away. When she looked back, the man was striding toward Hunt and the female detective. Then he stroked a proprietary hand down the woman's back. It was quick, but firm.

Hmm, so the woman wasn't after Hunt.

Not that it mattered.

"Savannah?"

Hunt and the couple moved her way.

"This is Detective Brynn Sullivan," Hunt said.

"I'm both his colleague and his cousin," Brynn said with a smile.

Hunt gestured. "And this is my friend, Vander Norcross."

The dark-haired man nodded. He wasn't a cop then, but he was *something*.

Savannah cleared her throat. "I'm Savannah."

"Did you see the shooter?" Brynn asked.

Savannah shook her head. "Hunt leaped on me. I didn't see anything."

The couple swiveled to glance at Hunt.

"Did you hear anything?" Vander asked.

"Just the shots. Lots of people screaming and crying." She let out a shuddering breath, then glanced at the bullet marks on the floor again.

"What is it?" Hunt asked.

Damn, the man could read her so quickly and easily. She shook her head. "I... It's just all the bullets are in one area."

Hunt frowned.

"Looks like the shooter was just targeting the center of the store," Brynn said.

"Right." That had to be it.

"I'll get statements from those near the windows," Brynn said. "Maybe someone saw the make and model of the vehicle. We're also pulling any CCTV." She smiled. "It was nice to meet you, Savannah, even under these circumstances."

Vander Norcross nodded, but his gaze shifted back to the bullet holes.

"You look spooked," Hunt said to Savannah.

"We just got shot at." She rubbed her arms. "I'm entitled to be spooked." She bit her lip. "So many people could have been hurt or killed."

"Luckily, they weren't." He cocked his head. "Are you in trouble, Savannah?"

"What? *No.*" She shook her head. "No. This is nothing to do with me." She prayed that was true.

He eyed her, then nodded. "Come on, I'll drop you home."

"I have my bike."

"I can fit it in the back of my car."

"Hunter—"

His gaze locked on hers. "I'm taking you home, Savannah. No arguments."

CHAPTER FIVE

At the end of a long day, Hunt pulled up in front of the converted warehouse in South Beach.

Vander had gutted the inside of the brick warehouse and renovated it. The bottom level was parking for the company's fleet of cars, a well-equipped gym, and some holding rooms. The main level was open plan, with glass-walled offices. The upper level, with a roof terrace, was Vander and Brynn's loft.

Hunt pressed the buzzer at the front door, then scraped a hand down his face. Disrupted sleep, the coffee shop shooting, followed by a day where it felt like every one of his cases had hit a snag, had left him running on fumes.

He'd texted Savannah to check on her earlier.

How are you doing?

Who is this?

You know who it is. You doing okay?

How did you get my number?

I'm a cop, remember?

There'd been a long pause.

Isn't it against the law to just access someone's number?

No.

It should be. I'm okay. I'm painting. You okay?

Not the first time I've been shot at.

She'd sent him a shocked-face emoji.

The door clicked open in front of him, snapping him out of his thoughts. He strode into the Norcross Security offices.

Inside was all metal and glass, with a strong industrial vibe. Most people had left for the day, but he followed the murmur of voices into the domain of Norcross Security's tech guru.

Screens covered all the walls, and three men were taking up most of the space. Ace Oliveira sat in a chair in front of the desk, long legs stretched out in front of him. He was tall and lean, with his long, black hair tied in a ponytail. The ex-NSA Red Team hacker didn't look like a geek.

Vander stood beside him, eyeing the screens, more relaxed than Hunt had ever seen the former Ghost Ops commander. Vander had been one of the best of the best of special forces. He'd run the covert team for years, doing some of the toughest missions in the hardest places in the world.

But he'd known when to get out, before the hard, dangerous work eroded too much of his soul, or killed him.

Now, he ran Norcross Security, doing his bit to keep the streets of San Francisco safe. There was no doubt that Hunt and Vander butted heads on a semi-regular basis, and Hunt had to clean up after the Norcross men occasionally, but Vander was Hunt's friend. He knew Vander was a good man, and did good work.

And now that Vander had fallen in love with Brynn, he'd seen that his cousin had soothed some parts of Vander's scarred soul.

The remaining man looked up and smiled at Hunt.

Okay, it wasn't exactly a smile, just a lift of the corner of his mouth.

"Hey, big brother," the man said.

"Camden," Hunt said.

His brother's green eyes were watchful and flat. He had a newly healed scar that ran down his cheek, and that alert, still-in-combat aura to him. Hunt kept his face blank. It would fade. He knew, because he'd looked the same when he'd first gotten out of Delta. His brother was surrounded by family and friends, good people. He'd be fine.

"Now, why would one of San Francisco's finest be gracing us with his presence?" Ace drawled. The tech man lifted an apple and bit into it.

"Hi, Ace. How's Maggie?"

The man smiled. "Gorgeous, and very pregnant. I'm enjoying the ride that is pregnancy hormones."

Ace had gotten tangled up with Norcross' helicopter pilot, and gotten her pregnant in the process. After a bumpy courtship, they were both happily engaged and waiting for the arrival of their baby.

"How can we help, Hunt?" Vander asked.

Hunt stuck his hands into his pockets. He'd had a niggle at the back of his neck ever since he'd dropped a shaken Savannah back at her place. He could see that she was chewing on something about the shooting. She'd been shaken that others could've been hurt or killed.

He suspected she knew something.

If she was in danger, he needed to know.

"I need Ace to run a search on my new neighbor."

Cam's brows went up. "Your smoking-hot, blonde neighbor? The one you called dibs on?"

Hunt shot him a bland look.

"Ryder called me," Cam said, with a shrug.

"Savannah?" Vander asked.

Hunt nodded. "I ran a quick search. She's clean. Too clean."

Vander frowned. "You think she's into something bad?"

"No. I think she has trouble and she's running from something bad. "

"You ask her?"

"She clammed up. She's housesitting, claims she's not staying long. She moves around a lot."

Vander crossed his arms over his chest. "She won't thank you for digging into her past."

"If it keeps her safe, I don't care."

Vander nodded.

Ace's fingers were already dancing across the keyboard. "Name. Any details you have."

"Savannah Cole." Hunt repeated the details he'd uncovered about her.

Ace whistled. He had a picture of Savannah up. It was from her driver's license, but she'd avoided the usual horrible photo thing and still looked fresh and beautiful.

Cam nodded. "I see the attraction."

Hunt felt a shot of irritation at his brother's admiring tone. He grunted.

"Cool it, bro, I know you called dibs." A half-smile hit Cam's lips.

"She's clean." Ace spun in his chair and smiled. "Her ID is also fake. But it's a damn good fake. Her history goes back ten years. Savannah Cole, graphic designer, didn't exist before that."

Hunt sucked in a breath. "Who is she?"

"I don't know. That will take more digging. Whoever set up Savannah Cole did a great job."

"Can you find out who?" Vander asked.

"I can try." Ace flexed his hands. "I'll set up some searches, but then I need to head home to my baby mama."

Hunt rubbed the back of his neck and nodded. "Call me if you find anything."

Ace saluted.

Vander lifted his chin, and Cam clasped Hunt's shoulder. "See you at Mom's for lunch on Sunday."

"Yeah." Their mom liked to feed her boys as often as they'd let her.

Hunt drove home. As he passed, he saw that the Bean's windows were boarded up. He'd checked on the man who'd been shot earlier, too. He was fine, and already discharged.

As Hunt pulled to a stop outside his place, he saw the light was on in Savannah's bedroom. He wondered what she was working on.

As he walked upstairs, he turned on the lights and loosened his tie. It was nice to be home. He debated having a beer, versus going straight to bed.

Bed won.

He took a quick shower and pulled on some loose, gray sleep shorts. He dropped onto his bed, and watched the shadows dance on the ceiling.

A faint buzzing sound came through the wall. He frowned. The soundproofing in the townhouses wasn't bad, but as proven by Savannah's love for rock 'n roll, sound still got through.

What the hell was the buzzing? Some artist's tool?

Then realization hit him.

Savannah's *bedroom* was just on the other side of the wall.

He heard a woman's soft cries, and he stiffened. So did his cock.

Savannah was using a toy. And it had nothing to do with artwork.

Fuck.

He shoved the sheet off his overheated body. Another

sweet cry and Hunt cursed again. He shoved his shorts down and took his cock in hand.

He imagined Savannah on the bed, *his* bed, her legs spread and blonde curls spilling everywhere. He tugged on his cock and his breathing sped up. Desire was like lightning down his spine.

Through the wall, he heard more moans and cries.

With a brutal grip, he jerked his cock harder, faster. Then he heard one distinct word.

"*Hunter.*"

Shit. With another hard jerk, Hunt cursed and came, spilling on his gut. He groaned through the pleasure.

He lay there, spent, breathing heavily. *Fuck.*

It was the best orgasm he'd had in a long time.

There was no sound from next door, now. Shaking his head at just how worked up Savannah Cole had him, he headed to the bathroom to clean up.

He returned to his bed, back in his sleep shorts. Now music thumped from next-door. He rolled his eyes and plumped the pillow under his head. She couldn't help herself. Thankfully, it wasn't cranked quite as high as usual.

Strangely, he found it comforting.

Then he heard a loud thud. He frowned. There was another thud.

Like someone had knocked something over.

Another thud.

Hunt sat up. Then he heard another noise. A woman's muffled scream, quickly cut off.

Fuck.

He snatched up his SIG and charged out of his room.

THE MAN'S weight hit her again.

Savannah's easel crashed to the floor. He was big, wearing all black clothes and a balaclava over his face.

They spun, knocked over a chair, and went down.

Her heart was racing. Fear and panic crashed together inside her like paint splashed on the floor. She hit the floorboards hard, the man on top of her.

Savannah grunted. "Leave me—"

Gloved hands clamped on her neck and squeezed.

No. *No.*

Adrenaline shot through her. She didn't want to fucking die. She kicked her legs, her feet hammering on the floor. She'd fought so damn hard to stay alive and protect her family.

The man squeezed harder. The pain was horrible, she couldn't breathe. She reached out, trying to grab something, anything, but there was nothing in reach.

Wait. She still had the paintbrush that she'd stuck in her hair earlier. She reached up, her lungs burning.

Her fingers closed on the well-worn wood, and she yanked it out. Black splotches appeared in her vision.

Dark eyes stared down at her, showing no emotion.

Fuck you. She rammed the end of the paintbrush at his eye.

He turned at the last minute, but she still clipped him.

He muttered a curse, and his hands loosened. Savannah drew a breath into her oxygen-starved lungs.

But the guy kept her pinned under his larger body.

He recovered quickly, gripped her neck again, and rapped her head against the floor.

Savannah saw stars. Her consciousness wavered.

No. If she blacked out, she'd be dead.

Those strong fingers squeezed.

She thought of her mom and brother. *I miss you so much. I love you.*

She thought of Hunter. Of never having the chance to paint him, taste him, touch him. Hunter's strong hands protected, they didn't kill.

In the distance, she heard a crash.

Her attacker tensed.

Then she saw a flash of movement, and the man's weight lifted off her.

Panicked, she sat up and scrambled backward. She touched her sore throat, sucking in short, sharp breaths.

Two men were wrestling on the floor—one wearing black clothes, and one in shorts with his broad back bare, just smooth bronze skin.

Hunt.

Savannah leaned back against the couch. Her heart hammered so hard against her chest she thought it would burst out. She was lightheaded, and she tried desperately not to pass out.

She heard the thuds of knuckles on flesh, and deep masculine grunts. The man in black jumped up. Hunt did as well, swiveled, and tripped the guy.

There were more grunts, then her attacker managed to get to his feet and ran. She saw him sprint down the stairs, slamming into the railing as he went.

A bare-chested Hunt ran after him.

Then she was alone.

Panic closed in. What if the attacker wasn't alone? Her mouth went dry, her vision blurred.

She fought to slow her breathing. She couldn't pass out.

She heard heavy footsteps coming back up the stairs.

Panic burned like acid in her veins. She snatched some scissors off the coffee table and held them up.

Hunt appeared and headed straight for her.

When he reached her, she dropped the scissors. They clattered on the floor. She flew into his arms.

As his arms closed around her, she burrowed into him. She felt warm male skin, smelled Hunt.

He sat on the couch and pulled her onto his lap.

God. *God.* She burrowed deeper, her face pressed against his neck. When was the last time someone had held her?

When was the last time someone had made her feel safe?

"He got away?" she asked shakily.

"He got away. He ran off into the night, and I didn't want to leave you unprotected."

She breathed in his skin. His hand curved around her hip and tightened.

"You get a look at him?"

"No. His face was covered." She swallowed. Her throat was sore and her voice was hoarse. "He had dark eyes. He was big."

Hunt grunted. "I need to call it in."

She gripped onto him tighter. "Can you...do it in another minute?"

"Okay, baby." He hugged her tighter and stroked a hand down her back. "You didn't know him?"

Her stomach did its best to scrunch into a tiny knot.

Andrew Walkson, her stalker, was the same height as her. He had a slim build, but she'd learned that he was still strong. She knew very well that men were stronger, even when they didn't have a big, muscular build.

It had not been Andrew Walkson choking her.

"I've no idea who that man was. It had to be a random attack, right? Some crazy?"

Hunt grunted. His hands stroked her back soothingly. Then he reached up and touched her collarbone. As he looked at her neck, she watched his face darken. Something dangerous moved through his eyes.

"I'm okay," she assured him.

"No, you're not. You need to go to the hospital."

"No! No hospital."

He frowned. "You want to tell me why?"

Because of the paperwork. A trail that Walkson could follow. Plus, she hated the hospital. She spent terrifying hours in one, after she'd survived Walkson's attack.

"Because."

"Savannah—"

She pressed a hand to his jaw. His stubble was rough under her fingers. "Hunter, please."

He released a breath. "Fine, but I'm calling this in, then calling my brother."

"The hot paramedic?"

"I'd prefer you didn't notice or mention that first part."

Despite the circumstances, she smiled. "I noticed his hot cop brother first."

Hunt kissed her lips gently. "Good."

Her heart squeezed. Alarm bells were ringing in her head, very loudly. She needed to run.

She needed to get away from here, from this man.

She listened as he called in the attack, then had a short conversation with his brother, who didn't seem fazed about coming out in the middle of the night.

Every instinct told her to bolt and not look back.

But Savannah didn't run. She didn't move. Instead, she held on to Hunter and snuggled deeper into his big, strong body.

For now, just for a little while longer, she'd stay and absorb the sense of safety he generated. The sense of someone giving a shit about her.

Just for tonight.

CHAPTER SIX

The officers had arrived quickly, and Hunt took them through the events of the evening as they all walked through Savannah's place.

"Looks like he picked the lock on the front door," Officer Charles said. "Did a good job of it, too. There's little damage."

Hunt grunted. He looked across Savannah's living room. She was curled in the corner of the couch while Ryder finished checking her over.

Just the sight of the growing bruises on her neck was enough to stir Hunt's slowly simmering rage.

"I don't think we'll get any prints," Officer Charles added.

"No," Hunt agreed. "The asshole wore gloves."

"Well, we'll run a check for any similar attacks and let you know. Sorry this happened to her."

"Thanks, Charles."

Hunt saw the officers out. Then he moved over to the couch.

Those turbulent, gray eyes locked on him.

As she watched him, she took a deep breath and relaxed a little. It was like she needed to see him to stay calm. He liked knowing that because he was there, it steadied her.

Fuck if that wasn't a good feeling.

"She needs rest," Ryder said. "We've iced her neck. The painkillers will take the edge off. There's nothing broken or damaged, so time will do the rest."

"Thanks, Ryder," Hunt said.

"Sure thing, bro." Ryder met his gaze. *You've got this?*

I've got this.

Ryder gave him a chin lift. *Keep her safe.*

After Hunt's brother packed up his black bag, he gently touched a finger to Savannah's cheekbone, then headed out.

Savannah curled into a tighter ball. "I don't know why someone would do this. That asshole!"

It was nice to see some color in her cheeks.

She looked scared, mad, and frustrated all mixed together. She looked up at him and tucked a curl back behind her ear. "Thanks, Hunter. If you hadn't come in..." She looked at the floor.

The bastard would've killed her. Hunt's gut went tight. "You're moving in with me."

Her head jerked up, her eyes popped wide. "What?"

"You aren't safe alone. I'll board up the door for tonight, then call someone to repair it tomorrow."

"So I'll stay with you just for tonight?"

"No. Until I'm satisfied you're safe. You have any idea who'd target you?"

She looked away, staring blindly out the window.

"Savannah?"

She looked back, wary.

"You know I'm a detective?" he said.

She nodded.

"I know when someone's lying, or not telling me the entire truth."

She bit her lip, then pulled in a deep breath. "I swear that I don't know that man who attacked me. I promise you."

Damn, Hunt believed her. "But there's another one out there, who's after you."

She looked away again, shoulders slumping. She looked so tired.

Hunt felt a violent urge to not only protect her, but to look after her. "Come on. Let's grab some clothes, and whatever else you're going to need at my place."

She rose and moved to the stairs up to her bedroom. He followed her, and when she stopped at the door to her room abruptly, he tensed.

"Um, I can pack some things myself—"

"I'm not leaving you alone." He reached past her and snapped the light on.

He figured she'd left it messy. Maybe she had underwear strewn all over the floor?

Instead, he saw the large canvas leaning against the wall and froze.

It was stunning, and erotic as hell. It was done in a fascinating style, with daubs of paint, giving it a dreamy quality. A man, still clothed, holding a naked, blonde woman. Her sensuous body was tipped back, his mouth at her breast.

Fuck. It was *him.* And Savannah.

She made a beeline to the closet, avoiding looking at him. Hunt stared at the painting. It was beautiful, sexy. His cock stirred.

He wanted it.

Like how he wanted Savannah Cole.

But right now, he needed her safe.

She came back with a large, black overnight bag.

"I want to buy the painting," he said.

"It's not for sale."

"It's mine. And we both know it." He took the bag from her.

"It's not you," she said.

"Don't lie," he said. "You need anything else?"

She looked lost. She touched her throat and winced.

The sight of her developing bruises stirred his rage and protective instincts again. He wanted that fear and uncertainty off her face. She needed a distraction.

"What about your toy?" he asked.

She blinked. "My what?"

He waved to the bedside table. "Your toy. I heard you use it. My bed is on the other side of that wall."

"*What?*" It wasn't quite a screech, but it was close. Color filled her cheeks.

Yep, that was much better than the fear and worry.

She stalked over to him, and tried to grab her bag. "What I do in my own bedroom is none of your business, Detective. Now, give me the bag. I'll carry it."

"No."

They briefly played tug-of-war, then, with a frustrated noise, she let the bag go.

"Fine, carry it then." She stomped out and down the stairs.

He followed. In the living area, she snatched up her sketchbook, and a tin he guessed held paints and pens.

She radiated annoyance as they made their way downstairs.

But as they passed through her broken front door, her annoyance faded. He hated the frightened look in her eyes. He pressed a hand to the nape of her neck.

"You're safe."

"I'm never safe," she whispered.

He gently squeezed, until she looked at him. "You're safe with me."

They stared at each other, then she pulled in a shuddering breath.

He saw how exhausted she was. "Come on."

He led her into his place. In his kitchen, he put the kettle on, while she curled up on his couch. He made a mug of tea and brought it over.

"You don't seem like a tea kind of man," she said.

"My mom left it here." He resisted the urge to stroke Savannah's hair. "I'll go and deal with your door."

He saw the flash of fear at the idea of being alone, but she reeled it in. After another couple of seconds, she nodded.

"Stay here. I won't be long."

That got him another nod.

He got what he needed from his garage, and dealt with boarding up Savannah's front door. He paused.

Fuck. If he hadn't heard the noises, if she'd played her music louder...

She was okay. He had to remind himself of that. He headed back upstairs to find her curled in a ball on the couch, asleep.

She'd untied her hair, and the golden, loose curls spilled everywhere. He sat beside her and touched one of those silken curls.

Shit. What was this woman doing to him? He suddenly realized that he could happily sit here and watch her sleep soundly and safely.

That wasn't stalker-ish at all. He scooped her up and her eyes snapped open.

"It's okay," he murmured. "I'm taking you to bed."

"Hunter." Her body relaxed and her eyes drifted closed again.

Warmth filling his chest, he carried her upstairs, then hesitated at the door to the guest room.

The bed wasn't made. Yeah, it was a lame excuse, but totally legit. He wanted her in his bed. Wanted her close.

In the shadowed master bedroom, he set her down on the bed.

Her hand shot out. "Don't go. Please."

"I won't, baby. I'm right here."

He climbed in and wrapped his body around hers. "Sleep now."

SAVANNAH WOKE UP, then froze. She had no idea where she was.

Her pulse jumped like a frightened cat.

She heard steady breathing, and felt a hard, very male body behind her. It was wrapped protectively around her.

Hunter.

She barely knew him, but she'd know the feel and smell of him anywhere.

The events of the night rushed back at her. *God.* She swallowed. Her throat was sore, and she touched it gently and winced.

Hunt came awake like he hadn't even been asleep. "You in pain?"

All Savannah could see in the morning light peeking around the blinds was his bare chest. A huge expanse of bronze skin over hard muscles. The detective did not conform to any sort of doughnut-eating-cop stereotype.

He had sleek muscles everywhere—ridges down his abdomen that begged to be traced, along with a little happy trail of brown hair. And she really, really wanted to explore the ink on his left arm. It was the only part of him that was tattooed.

She would never have picked Detective Hunter Morgan to have ink under his sensible suits.

"Savannah?"

She tore her gaze off him. "It hurts a little."

"Here." He reached for something on the bedside table, then held out pills and a glass of water.

She swallowed the pills with a grimace, then lay back on the pillows.

Hunt lay down beside her, propped up on one arm, which made the muscles in his bicep flex.

She swallowed a groan.

Then, those long, strong fingers she'd admired, stroked her neck. Gently. So gently.

"The bruises look terrible," he said.

"Great," she muttered.

He stroked higher. "When I catch the asshole..."

Pure rage vibrated through his voice. Shit, what would he do to the guy? She didn't want Hunt to get into any trouble.

"Hunter—"

"Shh." He shifted, moving over her. His lips brushed her bruises.

Oh, God. Warmth flashed through her body. How long had it been, since anyone had touched her like this, since anyone had cared about her?

Tears pricked her eyes. He kept laying butterfly-like kisses on her neck. She slid a hand into his brown hair and arched her head back. Such a small touch, but she felt it all the way through her body.

"I hate seeing these bruises on you," Hunt murmured. "I hate knowing he hurt you, and that if I hadn't have heard, hadn't have been fast enough, he might've—"

"Hey." She tugged his head up. God, he was handsome. Not in that clean-cut, movie star way. No, Hunt was rugged, all-male. "You saved me." Tears threatened. Horrified, she dashed them away. "God, why am I crying?"

His hands pressed either side of her, his face close. "I don't know. Why?"

The emotions in her coalesced. She'd been alone and

scared for so long now. This rugged, protective man cared. For some reason, she mattered. It hit her right in the heart.

"Because you give a shit. No one has for a long time. Because I hate being scared." Tears rolled down her cheeks. "Because I never cry."

He pulled her against his chest. She pressed her cheek to his pec, and pulled in a shuddering breath.

"So cry. I've got you." His arms closed around her, his deep voice rumbled under her ear.

She knew she shouldn't. She knew that leaning on him, something that felt so good, would hurt more in the long run when she didn't have it anymore.

But the tears fell. She couldn't stop them.

She clung to Hunt and sobs welled up.

Savannah let her grief loose. Grief at everything she'd lost, everything that had been taken from her: safety, security, a chance to share her art, her family, life, love.

She wept against Hunt and one big hand cupped the back of her head. He held her tight. Right here, right now, she was safe. She didn't have the strength to pull away from him.

Finally, the storm ended. She rested against him.

"If you trust me, Savannah, I can help you."

She squeezed her eyes close. No, he couldn't. Her stalker was too cunning and too dangerous.

"Sorry to cry all over you."

Hunt sighed, and stroked her back. "Go and have a hot shower. I'll make you some breakfast."

She pulled back and swiped her cheeks. "For a man, the tears didn't seem to rattle you too much."

He shrugged a shoulder. "Tears, especially female ones, used to panic me. I only have brothers, remember? But I've been in the job too long now, and I've seen a lot of people cry."

Her belly clenched. He'd probably seen plenty of weeping women.

His fingers brushed her jaw. She felt it down to her toes.

"But something tells me yours are a gift. One you've never shared with anyone."

Danger. She bit her lip. *Danger, danger*. The man was one giant risk to her: mind, body, and soul.

"I'll hit the shower," she said.

He nodded. "You're coming with me to the station today."

She blinked. "What?"

"Until I'm satisfied that you aren't in danger."

"I can't just hang at the station."

He rose, big and handsome, and that bare chest with a light covering of dark hair was distracting. "I'm not letting you out of my sight."

"Hunt—"

"You call me Hunter," he growled.

She pulled in a deep breath. "Hunter, what will I do at the station all day?"

"Bring your sketchbook. Your paints. I'll be following up on your attack." He tilted his head. "You're sure you don't know who it was or why they attacked you?"

It hadn't been Walkson. "I truly have no idea."

Hunt waited a beat, then nodded. "I'll shower in the guest bathroom, and then meet you in the kitchen."

He stalked out, and her gaze dropped to his muscular ass clad in those loose shorts. Finally, she dragged herself into the bathroom. It was as neat and tidy as the rest of Hunt's place. The mirror informed her that she had dark circles under her eyes, but she barely noticed them, thanks to the bruises on her neck.

Holy cow. She stroked the skin there—it was purple and black. *Ugh.* At least thanks to the pain pills, she wasn't hurting much.

Right, shower time, then breakfast. If she took too long, her bossy detective would come looking for her. She turned on the shower.

He's not yours, Savannah.

He will never be yours.

She stepped under the water.

If he isn't mine, why am I naked in his shower after sleeping with him half the night?

She pressed a hand to the tiles. *Shut up, brain.*

But Savannah was far more worried about her heart.

She had to leave soon, and the thought of never seeing Hunter Morgan again—never knowing the feel of his hands, the taste of his skin, the thrust of his cock—it hurt.

She groaned. She had to leave. Soon.

CHAPTER SEVEN

Hunt couldn't dispute the fact that he liked seeing Savannah curled up in the guest chair in front of his desk.

The police station was in the Public Safety Building in the Mission District. It was a few years old, done in a modern style, with lots of glass and concrete. Unlike some of the other detectives, he kept his office sparse and his desk clean.

The only knickknack he had was a paperweight shaped like a police badge that Brynn had given him for his birthday one year. Outside, phones were ringing, and voices were raised in multiple conversations. There was always action around the detective offices.

He'd watched Savannah absorb it all as they passed through. She'd explored his office in thorough detail.

"I was expecting mismatched furniture and stained linoleum," she said.

"You've watched too many old cop shows on TV. The

city built this place a few years ago to house the police station, fire department, and arson team."

"It's fancy."

His cell phone rang, and he saw it was Vander. He held up a finger and pressed the phone to his ear. "Hi, Vander."

"I'm incoming with Ace."

Hunt stiffened. "You found something?"

"A whole stinking pile of something. You know she's wanted for questioning about a murder?"

Hunt's hand clenched. "No." He felt hot, then cold. His gaze shot to her—small, delicate, beautiful.

Savannah a murderer? Every instinct in him screamed that it was a lie.

But was he too close to make the judgment?

"It stinks to high heaven, Hunt. Some things are off about it. Wait, Ace has something else. You know she has a stalker?"

Hunt ground his teeth together, his eyes on the curve of her jaw. "I suspected something like that."

"Hold tight, and we'll share when we get to you."

"Roger that." Hunt slipped the phone away. "I have a meeting. Don't leave this office."

She saluted him. "Aye, aye, captain."

"Smart ass." He touched her cheekbone, because he couldn't stop himself. He saw the spark in her eyes.

If she was a killer, he'd turn in his badge. He wished she'd confide in him though.

"I'll be back," he told her.

He took a moment to organize a meeting room, and

soon Ace and Vander strode in. Hunt watched a female officer do a double take at the men. Vander was wearing a suit, and Ace was in suit pants, with a checked shirt with the sleeves rolled up, and a laptop bag slung over one shoulder.

Hunt waved them into the room and closed the door.

"Savannah was attacked last night," he said.

Vander's face darkened. "What happened?"

"Intruder at her house. Tried to choke her. I intervened, but the asshole got away."

"How is she?" Vander asked.

"Bruised." Just the thought of those marks again shot anger through Hunt's veins. "She's not a fucking killer. I arrest killers for a living."

Vander sat as Ace opened the laptop on the conference table.

"We all know that the right circumstances can cause anyone to take a life." Dark shadows stirred in Vander's eyes. "But no, I don't think your woman is a killer."

Hunt's hand flexed. "She's not mine... Yet."

Ace snorted. "Where did she sleep last night?"

Hunt stayed silent.

"She staying with you now?" Vander asked.

Hunt nodded.

Ace turned to the big screen at the end of the room and tapped his keyboard. "This is what I dug up. It was hard to find because it was buried deep. Her new name was generated by someone with talent. It would've cost a pretty penny." A picture of Savannah's driver's license flashed up. "Savannah Cole's background goes back ten years, but it's only been active for the last four."

Hunt frowned. "Someone created it four years ago, but went back and laid a trail for ten?"

Ace nodded. "Most people only go back a few years. Prior to four years ago, she was Susannah Hart."

Pictures from some sort of party at an art gallery popped up on the screen.

Savannah's hair was shorter, more silvery-blonde. Her smile... Hunt's chest hitched. It was wide and open. She looked happy, not guarded.

"She was an up-and-coming artist in New York City," Ace said.

Fuck. Hunt pressed his hands to the table. "What happened?"

"A young, blonde artist named Amelia Kerry was found dead in the gallery after Susannah Hart's showing. She was also an up-and-coming artist, a rival of Susannah's." The next images were crime scene shots.

Vander's face didn't change, Ace winced, and Hunt's lips flattened. It was brutal and bloody.

"Susannah Hart's prints were everywhere, including on the knife beside the body."

"She had an alibi?" Hunt asked.

"She said she'd been held by a madman. An art admirer who'd been stalking her. She'd reported him before. NYPD hadn't been able to track the threatening letters and gifts down to anybody."

"But?" Hunt prompted.

"She was covered in cuts. The police surmise that they could have been defensive wounds."

"Any pictures?"

Ace shook his head. "Then Susannah Hart disappeared."

"And Savannah Cole was born," Vander continued. "She moves around, rarely stays anywhere long."

Hunt nodded. "She's currently housesitting."

Vander crossed his arms. "No lease or bills in her name."

"Someone attacked her. And likely shot at her at the coffee shop." Hunt had connected the dots.

"Maybe Amelia Kerry's family? After revenge?" Ace suggested.

Hunt growled. "Savannah did *not* kill that woman."

The man looked at him steadily.

He cursed. "Don't tell me you think she did."

Vander leaned back in his chair. "Fuck, no. It took Ace an hour to find her stalker."

The image changed to show an unassuming man in his mid-twenties. He was smiling like life was good.

"Andrew Brandon Walkson. Art lover." There were candid shots of the man at the gallery, standing right behind Savannah.

"How come NYPD didn't nail him?" Hunt said.

Ace shrugged. "I ran every person from all of Susannah Hart's art shows, and focused on repeat customers who bought her artwork. Got hits on CCTV at her old apartment. This guy also has a juvenile record for stalking a girl at his high school. According to him, she was his girlfriend. She said they barely knew each other."

"How did you access a sealed juvie record?" Hunt shook his head. Ace was a top-notch hacker. "Never mind. Don't tell me."

Ace grinned, but then his smile dissolved. "Susannah Hart started getting gushing, creepy cards, letters, flowers. She ignored them. Then she started dating a guy, a stockbroker."

Hunt kept his face blank.

"When she did, the letters turned threatening. The police had no leads. Walkson bought a lot of her artwork, then she found one piece, broken, on her doorstep. Walkson said it was stolen. Then Susannah was allegedly attacked, and Amelia Kerry was murdered."

"And Savannah ran. And she hasn't stopped. Where's Walkson now?"

"New York. He's an insurance salesman. Travels a lot."

A muscle ticked in Hunt's jaw. "Makes for good cover to stalk a woman on the run. Has he been here in San Francisco?"

"He was in LA recently, but not San Francisco. As far as I can tell, he's in New York."

"Why shoot up a coffee shop?" Vander asked. "Or get someone to break in and choke her? Does that fit this guy's profile?"

No. It didn't.

"I need to talk to Savannah," Hunt said.

He tried to control the emotions inside him. Usually, it wasn't a problem, but this mix of anger, rage, fear, and frustration was volatile.

He'd asked her if she was in danger, and she hadn't trusted him enough to tell him.

He looked at the open, pretty face of Susannah Hart. Could he really blame her?

"Thanks, Ace, Vander. I owe you."

"We'll keep digging on Walkson," Vander said.

The men rose.

Vander stopped by Hunt. "And you don't owe me anything. I know I owe you, for so many things."

"Including letting you touch my cousin," Hunt said dryly.

Vander's lips quirked. "I'll tell her you said that."

"Said what?" As though they'd summoned her, Brynn appeared in the doorway.

"Nothing, Detective." Vander tugged her close and kissed her. "Your cousin was just being protective."

"Overprotective." Brynn rolled her eyes. "He can't help himself. I'm living with the man, Hunt. You've got to let it go."

Hunt tugged on her ponytail. "Never. I need to talk with Savannah."

Brynn eyed his face and frowned. "Problem?"

"Yeah. I'll let Vander update you."

Hunt headed for his office.

It was time for some answers.

WIELDING HER PAINTBRUSH, Savannah slashed paint on the paper she'd spread out on top of Hunt's desk.

She'd sketched for a while, but the urge to paint had taken over.

She'd spread some plastic on his desk, rolled out a large sheet of paper, and gotten to work.

It was an impressionistic portrait of the police station.

People coming and going, leaving trails, like car lights at night.

She wished the cops in New York had helped her. She didn't blame them, though. They had rules to follow, and so many who needed help. Walkson had set things up to make it look bad for her. She shuddered.

Daubing some blue paint on the paper, her thoughts turned to Marcie. She wondered how the woman was doing. Savannah dipped her brush in the blue paint and swiped some more on the paper.

One person in the painting stood in the center of the chaos, like a rock in a river. So steady and strong.

Hunt was really turning into her muse. She'd painted the detective faceless, with his hands on his hips, tie askew and holster on. But he had Hunt's broad shoulders and long legs.

The office door opened.

She looked over her shoulder and saw Hunt in the doorway. He looked at his desk, and his mouth dropped open. His brows drew together.

"What the hell are you doing?"

"Brain surgery." She moved the brush, adding more strokes.

"On my desk?" He strode over.

"I covered it in plastic. It's fine."

He growled.

She turned. "You wanted me to come here. I needed to work."

"I thought graphic design was your job."

"It is, but I...needed to paint."

"Art is your true calling. You should have a showing."

Her belly curdled and she looked away. "No. It's just a hobby."

"We both know it's not just a hobby, Susannah."

Ice flowed over her, locking her chest. She turned slowly, unable to breathe. "What did you call me?"

A muscle ticked in his jaw. "I know that you're really Susannah Hart."

She backed up and shook her head. "No."

"Hey, take it easy." He held out a hand.

She couldn't be Susannah. If she was, she'd be dragged back to that horrible place. She'd be Andrew Walkson's victim.

Walkson would get her. Hurt her family.

"Susannah—"

"Don't call me that." Her vision swam.

Hunt studied her for a beat. "Savannah." He nudged her into a chair. "Head down. Just breathe."

She did as he ordered and clutched her paintbrush like it was a lifeline.

"I didn't kill her," she whispered.

Poor, poor Amelia. Nausea whirled. Would she get locked up? Walkson had said he could reach her, even in jail.

"I know you didn't kill her," Hunt said.

Savannah's head jerked up. "You do?" Her chest filled, impossibly tight.

He cupped her jaw. "I'm a cop, Savannah. I know killers." His face darkened. "We need to talk about Walkson."

She flinched.

"You said you didn't know your attacker."

"I didn't. The man who choked me was *not* Andrew Walkson. He was bigger. Believe me, I know." She gave a hysterical laugh.

"He hurt you," Hunt said quietly.

She shuddered. "Yes. But he hurt poor Amelia worse, then tried to frame me. And then he terrorized my family. My father died about a year before Walkson started sending me letters. We were all still grieving and finding our feet without Dad. Walkson threatened my mom and younger brother, Ezra." She bit her lip hard. "He told me in great detail just what he'd do to them." She'd had nightmares about it for months.

"Jesus."

She grabbed the front of Hunt's shirt with her free hand. "He's not sane, Hunt. He's obsessed." She swallowed. "Do you think the attack has to do with him?"

Hunt frowned. "I don't know."

"He must've hired someone." She gasped. "And for the shooting at the Bean." She leaped out of the chair, her paintbrush clattering to the floor. "God. He's found me, and a whole new way to terrorize me. I have to go."

Hunt grabbed her arms. "You're not going anywhere." His voice was a gritty growl.

"I have to. He'll hurt more people." *Oh, God.* What if Walkson hurt Hunt?

She couldn't let that happen.

"I have to go."

"*No.* We don't know it's him for sure. Let me help you."

She tried to pull away. "No!"

"Let me rephrase that. I'm *going* to help you."

"Hunter—" anger sparked "—you don't get to boss me around. I'm an adult. I've been protecting myself for a very long time."

"Not anymore."

She saw the stubborn glint in his gorgeous green eyes.

Argh. He was going to dig in.

"You aren't listening. Andrew Walkson is dangerous."

"So am I."

His tone made her pause. She knew he was, but Walkson was sneaky. He wouldn't take Hunt head-on. He'd hide in the shadows, behind fake smiles and his ordinary face, and attack from behind.

She had to protect Hunt, but he wasn't listening. She made a strangled sound. "Don't go bossy on me." She shoved against his chest.

And splattered blue paint all over his white shirt.

She gasped, and saw him look down.

Suddenly, laughter bubbled up inside of her. "There goes another shirt, and it's totally your fault."

He made a sound, part growl, part something else. "I think it's your fault, and you owe me two new shirts."

She shook her head. "You brought it on yourself."

He reached out and dipped his fingers in the paint pots on his desk. Then he smeared his fingers over her face.

Savannah gasped. "You did *not.*"

His lips twitched and she reached past him, dipped her fingers in red, then swiped at his face. He tried to dodge, but she got him, smearing color on his collar.

Then it was war.

They both went at the paint. Savannah got green, and pressed handprints all over his shirt, and started laughing.

His paint-covered hand grabbed her shirt and hauled her in.

She hit his chest and gripped his arms.

They looked at each other for a beat, then their mouths collided.

Oh. *God.*

Heat. Need. Lust.

It felt like a wild explosion. She pressed into him, trying to climb that big body of his.

He groaned deeply in his throat, intensifying the kiss. One hand clamped on her ass, and she slid both her hands into his hair. She wound her tongue against his, desperate for more of his taste.

Then the sound of a choked female laugh made Savannah blink.

Hunt lifted his head. They were both breathing heavily.

"Hunt, I didn't know you were a budding artist."

Savannah looked over. A highly amused Brynn stood in the doorway.

Then she looked back, and barely controlled her own laugh. Hunt had paint on his shirt, streaked on his face, and in his hair.

Savannah guessed she hadn't fared much better.

"Not a word," Hunt growled.

Brynn smiled. "That's going to be impossible."

"Quiet." His gaze moved to Savannah. "You *aren't* leaving."

She didn't respond.

He gripped her chin. "You aren't leaving. We'll sort out the stalker who's after you together."

Savannah trembled. She wanted it so much. To not be alone. To lean on someone who cared.

"You can't get hurt," she whispered.

"I won't." He yanked her in for a hug.

"Well, Hunt, you have paint in your hair," Brynn said. "And Savannah has a lovely handprint on her ass. So why don't the two of you get cleaned up, and I'll take you out for lunch? I want all the details on Savannah's stalker."

"And you think I'm bossy," Hunt muttered.

CHAPTER EIGHT

Hunt set the chicken in the sizzling pan. He checked the pasta that was boiling, then tipped more balsamic glaze onto the chicken.

"I never pegged you for a chef."

He turned. Savannah was sitting at the island, where he'd planted her. She was wearing a pretty dress made of a green, patterned fabric. It was short enough to show off those slim legs and the V-neck gave him tantalizing glimpses of smooth skin. She cradled a glass of wine, but had only had a few sips.

He wanted her to relax, but tension throbbed off her. He could see her chewing on the situation. He realized she probably always did. Life on the run from her stalker meant she'd always be thinking of Walkson. Always driven by one man—a murderer who was obsessed with her.

Hunt also knew she was fighting not to run. Not to head out the door and disappear.

His gut locked.

He dipped his spoon into the sauce, then held it up to her. "Open."

She licked the spoon and moaned. Which went straight to his cock.

"I'm a single man, I like to eat, and take out every night leaves you overweight and feeling like crap. So, I learned to cook." He smiled. "And the ladies are always impressed."

"I've not seen any ladies." She glanced away. "Not that I've been spying on you, or anything."

His smile widened. He nudged her legs apart and liked the way her chest hitched. Just one small touch from him and she always responded. He stepped between them.

"I've been busy with work, and my sexy neighbor has been keeping me awake."

"Because of my loud music. I know."

"That, too."

A dull flash of color filled her cheeks.

"I talked with Vander. We're organizing for you to always be protected during the day. At night, you'll stay here with me. I have a good security system. After dinner, I'll show you how to enter the code."

"Protected?"

"You can't always spend the day at the station." As much as he wanted that. "So, if I can't be with you, you'll have a bodyguard."

Her eyes went wide. "Bodyguard?"

"I'm running Walkson down. The asshole will make a mistake, and I'll nail him. Ace from Norcross is insanely good with computers and is helping."

She wrapped her arms around herself. "Walkson is smart and cunning. He looks so...ordinary. Everybody falls for it."

Hunt leaned closer. "Will you tell me? About his attack?"

She shook her head. "It's in the past."

"It's not. He's driving your future."

"I don't care about my future, as long as my family is safe."

"Your mom and brother."

She nodded.

He slid his hand up the side of her face. She leaned into him, but only for a second, before she pulled away.

She pasted on a fake smile. "Is dinner ready? It smells good and I'm starved."

"I will keep you safe, Savannah."

Endless gray eyes met his. She stroked his stubbled cheek. "And I'll keep you safe."

His muscles tensed. He clamped his hands on her thighs. "You *aren't* leaving."

She didn't say a word.

A timer dinged. Cursing under his breath, Hunt headed to the stove.

"Let's eat." She leaped off the island to set the table. She pulled things out of his drawers. "Oh, my God, you have napkins. The real cloth kind."

"My mom helped me furnish the place. I hate to burst your bubble, but I've never used those napkins."

She rolled her eyes. "Men."

"Savannah, about Walkson and having protection—"

"Can we drop it? For now?" Her eyes pleaded with him. "Let's just enjoy our dinner."

Hunt released a breath. "Yeah, okay."

They ate and he watched her get edgier, fidgeting in her seat. After dinner, he cleared the table, then came back and gripped her shoulders. She was so tense.

"What do you need?" he asked.

She dragged in a breath. "My sketchbook."

He got it for her, and she moved to the couch. As he cleaned the kitchen, he watched her with her charcoal, feverishly working on the paper.

He loved how absorbed she got. It was the only thing in the world for her right now. With the bombardment of information and stimulation these days, so many people had lost the ability to do that deep focus.

But as he stacked the dishwasher, he saw the quick glances she shot his way, her gaze lingering on his rolled-up sleeves.

Hunt hid his smile. Savannah Cole was going to be under him, in his bed, very soon.

He dropped down on the couch beside her, reaching for a stack of unopened mail that he'd brought up earlier.

Mmm, Savannah's cute, bare feet with painted nails looked a lot more enticing than junk mail and bills.

Instead, he grabbed her feet and pulled them onto his lap.

"Hey," she said.

"Relax." He started massaging.

"Oh." Her eyes fluttered. "Damn, that's good."

He worked his thumbs into the balls of her feet. She moaned.

Hell. His cock was half hard around her anyway. It didn't need much more encouragement.

She tried to keep sketching.

"What are you working on?" he asked.

"Whatever catches my interest."

He grabbed the sketchbook.

"Morgan! Give it back."

He held it without looking at it. "Can I see?"

She hesitated, then nodded.

Hunt flicked it open and heat shot straight to his gut. Unruly emotion filled him.

She'd been sketching *him*. In various poses.

Him, standing in the middle of a crowd, in a suit with his holster on. He looked very in charge.

Him, barefoot and shirt untucked, at the stove cooking.

Him, sprawled in a chair, a faint smile on his face.

The final one was his hands running over a woman's naked body. *Shit.* Desire hit hard. She hadn't sketched all of the woman, but the slim lines matched Savannah.

She fidgeted. "I'm an artist and you're a good subject. It doesn't mean anything."

He looked up. "We both know that isn't true."

"Hunt, we can't do this. It's a very bad idea." She set the sketchbook on the coffee table.

"You mean you're scared."

"Yes, damn you. For about a hundred different reasons."

When she moved to shift her feet, he grabbed her calves and dragged her across the couch toward him.

"Hunter—"

"I love it when you say my name like that. Breathy, needy."

Something flared in her eyes. "I do not sound breathy or needy."

Then she shocked the hell out of him by straddling him.

Damn. He really liked that. He clamped his hands on her hips.

"I bet I can make *you* sound breathy and needy," she said.

In about ten seconds. "You're welcome to try."

She pressed her tongue to her teeth and moved her hips, and accidentally knocked his mail off the couch.

A note fluttered to the floor, written in red ink.

You can't have her.

She's mine.

You're dead.

Every muscle in Hunt's body tensed.

Savannah turned frozen like ice. "No." She shook her head. "*No, no, no.*"

ALL SAVANNAH COULD HEAR WAS her heartbeat pounding in her ears.

Hunt slid off the couch and snatched up the note carefully, by one corner.

She couldn't see it now, but the words were seared into her brain.

Walkson liked to write in blood.

Her vision swam. Hunt strode to the kitchen and put

the note in a plastic Ziploc bag. She wasn't going to have a panic attack, dammit.

She sucked in a breath and rose.

"I'll have it processed," he said. "We might get a print."

She shook her head. "There won't be any. There weren't any on the old ones he sent me."

Hunt's green gaze was piercing. "He's *not* going to get to you."

She was more worried about Walkson getting to Hunt.

Hunt opened a cupboard. "I'll call it in, and I'll take the note to forensics in the morning." He pulled out a bottle. He splashed amber fluid into two glasses.

He brought one over to her.

"What's this?" She took the glass.

"God's gift to mankind." He sniffed the liquor. "Blanton Gold. Bourbon."

Her nose wrinkled. "I don't like bourbon." But she knocked hers back. She needed it.

Heat filled her cheeks as the alcohol hit her system. Hunt sipped his.

He seemed so calm.

"He's targeting you," she snapped.

Hunt sipped again. "Savannah, I'm a cop. I carry a gun. I'm former Delta Force. I'm no easy target. Walkson has made a big mistake this time."

She bit her lip. She had to leave. She'd known it all along. "He'll attack you when you least expect it. It's how he got me."

"Tell me."

She shook her head. The image of Hunt—big, gorgeous, dependable Hunt—lifeless and bloody, made her stomach revolt. She set her glass down on the coffee table with a click.

"Don't let him get in your head, Savannah."

"He's been there for years. Haunting me. He threatened my mom and brother. He killed a woman who looked like me. All because of *me*."

Hunt touched her leg. "It's not your fault. Walkson is to blame."

"How can you be so calm?" Her pulse skittered like crazy. "He's dangerous."

"I know. And I'm not calm."

There was a snap in his voice that jerked her head up. She saw the blazing fire in his eyes.

"Hunter—"

"I hate seeing you terrified. I hate knowing you feel you have to flee, that this asshole has control over your entire life."

With catlike speed, Hunt slammed his glass down on the coffee table so hard it cracked the glass. "You've had to hide your art, stay away from your family." He cupped her cheek. "Deny yourself the life you want to live."

Her pulse was still pounding, but different emotions rushed through her now.

Hunt leaned in, his fingers brushing her cheek. "I'm going to stop him. Whatever it takes."

The fear raced back in. "Hunter..."

He rose and pulled her up. He moved to the window, and wrapped his arms around her.

"I'm going to stop him." Hunt tugged her so her back

was pressed snugly to his front. He was so strong. Warmth poured off him. "You never have to be afraid again." He nuzzled her neck. "I hope he's out there, watching, seeing that I have you, and that I'm not letting you go."

Oh, God. Hunt's mouth traveled to the side of her neck. He nipped.

She arched into him blindly, staring out onto the empty street.

Hunt pulled her away from the window and back to the couch. He dropped down and pulled her onto his lap so that she straddled him again.

"You're so beautiful, Savannah. So is your art. I want you to be able to share your talent with the world."

Her chest locked. "Don't you dare make me cry."

He smiled darkly. "Maybe I can make you feel something else, instead." His mouth took hers.

She shouldn't do this. Shouldn't let this man get closer.

But as soon as his mouth touched hers, she didn't care. On a moan, she opened her mouth, slipping her tongue between his lips.

He groaned and grabbed the back of her head. His kiss turned harder, more ferocious.

Vicious arousal washed away every single thought from Savannah's mind. Hunt pulled her closer, one hand sliding into her hair, tugging hard.

She ground against him, feeling the steel-hard bulge under her. His cock pressed against the juncture of her thighs and her clit throbbed. Her panties were saturated.

Savannah put everything into the kiss. She licked,

nipped, her tongue dueling with his. She rocked on his lap as he plundered her mouth. His raw hunger throbbed off him.

God, she loved messing up this oh-so-steady detective. This could become addictive.

His hand cupped one of her breasts. She made a sound, pressing into his palm. She wasn't over endowed, but she knew her breasts weren't bad. He thumbed her nipple through her dress and her bra until it pebbled.

Then he bunched up the bottom of the dress and slid his hand under the fabric.

She froze.

His palm pressed to her belly, and she felt his gaze lock on her.

She couldn't look at him.

His fingers moved, tracing the ridges of scars on her belly. Every muscle in her body strung tight.

"He did this." Hunt's voice held a gritty edge.

She nodded.

"Eyes, Savannah. Now."

She looked up.

There was no horror, revulsion, or worse, fascination.

"These are signs you survived, baby, that's all."

"I... I don't want to take my dress off."

"That's okay. I can make you come with it on."

What? His hand shifted, bunching up in her dress. The air caught in her lungs.

"Hunter—"

"Shh." He kissed her again.

Soon, she was so lost in the kiss, that she lost track of

everything. Then she felt his big hand under the dress, between her legs.

As his fingers brushed her panties, she jumped.

He pushed the damp fabric aside and his fingers stroked her. He made a hungry sound. "So soft."

As he stroked her, her hips moved, her small cries escaping her lips.

He found her clit and rubbed it.

Savannah gripped his shoulders. "Oh, God."

He slid two fingers inside her.

She'd sculpted them, so she knew they were big. She enjoyed the stretch, panting at the pleasure. His thumb moved back to her clit.

"Ride my hand, baby. I want to watch you come."

She couldn't have stopped if she'd wanted to. She moved her hips, working herself on his fingers, sensation jolting through her.

"Hot, tight, slippery." He bit her bottom lip. "I can't wait to watch you take my cock, Savannah."

She cried out. A shock of pleasure rocketed through her, and she picked up speed, moving her hips wildly.

Her orgasm was building, and she felt like she was on the edge of the cliff, ready to fall. He kept up the pace, his fingers plunging into her, his thumb rubbing her clit.

"*Hunter.*" He pushed deeper and Savannah came.

As the climax crashed over her—strong and potent—her body clamped down on his fingers.

She heard her cries and her vision wavered.

Then Hunt pulled his fingers free and tipped them sideways on the couch. He pulled her tight against his chest and held her.

"What about you?" she whispered, trying to get her breathing under control.

"Later. Right now, I'm right where I want to be."

He kissed her and she shivered, still floating in bliss.

"And I've got you right where I want you."

She clung to him, but even feeling so good, resting in his arms, her fear wasn't far away.

This didn't change anything. She had to protect him.

She had to leave.

CHAPTER NINE

Savannah crouched by the edge of Hunt's bed, night shadows dancing on the wall.

After her earth-shattering orgasm, they'd dozed on the couch. Hunt had finally urged her into his bedroom, into one of his big T-shirts, and into his bed.

Once again, he'd curled around her. She thought it would be hard to sleep, but she'd drifted off, feeling warm and safe.

Until she'd dreamed of Andrew Walkson stabbing Hunt, over and over.

Blood. There'd been so much blood.

Savannah had woken on a terrified gasp.

She'd lain there, heart racing, until the nightmare had passed. But as she'd stared at the ceiling, listening to Hunt's even breathing, she'd been excruciatingly aware that her nightmare could become reality.

More than anything, she'd wanted to stay here, curled up in Hunt's arms. To let him shield her.

But she couldn't.

She hadn't known him long, but she knew he was a good man. He had brothers, family, and friends who loved him. He was courageous and he'd fought for his country, and now served his city.

She had to keep him safe.

With her gone, Walkson would chase her, and leave Hunt alone.

"Goodbye, Hunter," she whispered.

It almost tore her apart to rise and walk silently out of the bedroom.

She'd stealthily snuck out of the bed, dressed, and grabbed a few things. Her belly contracted, tears pricking her eyes. She had to leave her paintings, her sculpture. She was only taking a bag with some clothes. She knew that Hunt would take care of her art.

In the living area, she spotted her sketchbook and snatched it up. She could at least keep the sketches of Hunt that she'd done. She pressed the book to her chest and closed her eyes. It was something, at least.

A tear rolled down her cheek. She glanced up, then forced herself to move.

She spied his car keys on the counter, and sent a silent little apology to him. Stealing a police detective's car was not how she wanted to leave, but she'd make sure she left it somewhere where he could find it.

Clutching the keys, she crept down the stairs. He'd parked on the street, and a part of her was terrified to go outside.

What if Walkson was waiting?

She straightened. He wouldn't be right out the door. If he was close by, then he'd chase her, and she'd get her asshole stalker far away from the good man who was asleep upstairs.

She shut down the alarm, just as Hunt had showed her earlier, and slipped outside.

It was three AM. The street was eerie and empty. There was no movement anywhere.

She hesitated.

Damn. This hurt more than she'd thought. The painful ball in her chest made fresh tears spill down her cheeks.

She had to protect Hunt. She was doing the right thing. She had to protect all the people here on the street. None of them were safe from Walkson.

She hitched her bag up on her shoulder and headed toward the Charger. The locks bleeped and she winced. It sounded deafeningly loud in the quiet of the night.

She threw her bag in the backseat and slid into the driver's seat. She sat there for a second, then sucked in a breath and pressed the start button.

Nothing happened.

Her pulse jumped. *No.*

"Oh, no." She pressed the button again, then again.

The engine didn't even make a sound.

This couldn't be happening. She *had* to leave tonight.

A rap on the driver's side window made Savannah scream.

But it wasn't Walkson's plain, normal face staring back at her through the glass. It was Hunt's rugged, very-pissed-off face.

She unlocked the car, and he yanked the door open.

"Get out of the car, Savannah." He said the words in a clipped tone.

She swallowed. "I have to go—"

"Get out of the car, or I'll carry you out."

"You aren't listening to me! I have to go. I have to keep you safe."

He leaned in and she registered idly that he wasn't wearing a shirt. Their noses brushed.

"Get out of the car," he said again.

Savannah's hands flexed on the steering wheel. "You did something to the car."

"Yes." He grabbed her arm and hauled her out.

She started to argue, but she saw the way his gaze carefully swept the street. She realized that he was alert, cautious. It wasn't safe out here.

She let him pull her inside.

"I knew you'd run." He towed her upstairs.

"I don't want to," she cried. "But I don't have a choice."

At the top of the stairs, he whirled. "You do. You stay here, and you trust me to protect you. But you don't trust anyone, do you?"

"I trust you," she yelled. "But I know him. He'll never stop. He's obsessed, he's evil. I don't want you hurt. I... couldn't handle it." Her voice cracked.

Hunt cursed. He crossed to her and yanked her against him. She clung to him.

"I won't survive if he hurts you," she mumbled against his chest.

"He's not going to hurt me. And he's not going to hurt

you. I've put away worse bugs than Walkson." He stroked her back. "You're safe. I *will* put Walkson in a cage."

She clung to him harder. She wanted to believe that so badly.

He dropped into an armchair and pulled her down with him. She snuggled into him, tucking her head under his chin.

His hand slid over her belly, and his fingers spread.

"Tell me," he said.

She knew what he wanted. After sharing her ordeal with the police, and then having them doubt her and accuse her of murder, she'd never told anyone.

She trembled. "I'm not sure I can."

"I'll start. I was on a mission with my Delta Force team, in a rough, not-very-nice place. I had a bad parachute landing, and blew out my knee."

His tone was devoid of emotion. Savannah waited. She knew there was more. There was hard, resolute resignation in his voice.

"I drugged up and completed the mission, but I did irreparable damage to my knee. The doctors told me I couldn't be special forces anymore." He dragged in a deep breath. "And I didn't want a desk job."

"So, you came home."

"Yeah. It took me a while to acclimatize, but I decided to become a cop, like my father had been. He died of a stroke a few years back, but he was proud as hell. Luckily, I took to it."

Savannah pressed her cheek to his chest. She was unsurprised.

"I was just getting settled at SFPD when I got the call."

His dark tone made her tense. He smoothed a hand down her thigh.

"My old team had gone on a mission. It went FUBAR. Three of them, three of the best men I've ever known, died. They bled out on fucking sand, half a world away from their families."

She held on to him. "I'm so sorry, Hunt."

"I wasn't there. I'd had their backs for years, and I wasn't there when it counted."

She kissed his jaw. "It's not your fault. You're not all-knowing."

"And it's not your fault that Walkson is obsessed with you, or killed that woman."

Damn, he'd turned it around on her.

IT WAS hard to beat down the volatile mix of emotions stewing in him.

If Savannah had managed to leave, she would've run. She would've slipped through Hunt's fingers and disappeared. She was good at it.

He might never have found her.

He tightened his hold on her. Here he was, baring his battered soul to her.

He didn't talk much about his Delta Force buddies, or the ones he'd lost: Eric, Mitchell, and Manny. He rarely talked about the crushing guilt. Occasionally, after a few too many beers or Blanton, he and Ryder would talk. Ryder had his own scars, but his brother had an easier-going personality. He didn't dwell as much.

Sometimes, in the middle of the night, Hunt couldn't help but think of the friends he'd lost, their families. Once a year, he visited their widows, and took toys and gift cards for the kids. The kids were getting older, growing up without their fathers. Hell, some barely remembered their dads.

"Hunter." Savannah stroked his cheek. "Your friends' deaths are on the people who killed them. I'm sure you all knew the risks when you signed up."

Yeah. He'd been willing to give his life, if required. But Savannah hadn't signed up to be terrorized by a madman, her life torn to shreds.

Hunt toyed with the hem of her T-shirt. He felt her stiffen, then slowly, purposefully relax.

Her hand moved down and she lifted the soft fabric up, inch by inch.

He pulled in a breath, honored by her trust.

She sucked in a sharp breath. He explored the thin ridges on her belly, rage welling. The bastard had used a knife on her. The scars weren't bad, but he knew she felt the weight of them.

"You could have them removed," he said.

"They remind me. Every day." Her voice was a whisper. "To never relax my guard."

He nuzzled her hair. "Tell me."

"I had a showing. Amelia was there and caused a scene. She was jealous of my success. I didn't care. I was on cloud nine. I'd sold a ton of pieces, and not even a creepy fan like Andrew Walkson could darken my day."

"You knew him."

"A little. He was always at my showings and he'd bought some of my art. The first piece he bought was a painting of an endless forest of trees, done in my signature style. I'd called it *Infinity*." She dragged in a breath. "He asked me out for coffee a bunch of times and I always declined. He...stared a lot. He unsettled me." She shifted, lost in the memories. "I never imagined that he was dangerous. Then Amelia went missing." Her voice turned dull. "The next night, I stopped by the gallery. I got a message from the owner about a piece."

"But it wasn't the owner."

"No." She bit her lip, and her hand fisted.

Hunt caught her fist and uncurled her fingers. "You're not alone. I'm here."

"Walkson was waiting. He dragged me into the back room. He's stronger than he looks." She shuddered. "He tied me up, then cut off my dress. It wasn't sexual, per se. I don't think he could—" she gestured with her hand "—but he enjoyed my fear, my pain. He toyed with me, sliced me up. He was angry that I kept turning him down. He said we were meant to be together." She shuddered again. "There was so much blood, and it hurt so much. I screamed, but no one heard. He told me in excruciating detail what he'd done to Amelia." Savannah's voice hitched. "For me. He said that he'd killed her for me."

"No. That's him trying to get in your head. He did it for him."

She swallowed. "When the sun rose, he left. He'd loosened the ropes and I got free. I was in a bad way, and ended up in the hospital. My mom and brother were frantic when I hadn't come home. My father had died the year before. Heart attack." A faint smile hit her lips. "That man had loved his bacon." Her smile faded. "Mom was super-protective, and she was beside herself. My best friend, Saskia, had spent the night looking for me." Savannah rubbed the fingers of her free hand against her temple. "Then the police came, but instead of listening to my story, they questioned me about Amelia. They'd found her body, and a knife with my blood and fingerprints on it." She started shaking. "It was horrible. They accused me of working with Walkson to kill my rival." Tears flowed down her cheeks. "I was so scared, and in so much pain. They accused me of *working* with my *attacker*. I was terrified that they were going to arrest me."

Hunt stroked her hair. "They were doing their jobs." But he realized how traumatizing it must've been for her.

"They were relentless, even after I was released from the hospital. They couldn't find Walkson. Then..." She pressed a hand to her belly.

Hunt tensed and knew there was more to come.

"Walkson sent me a note. It included photos of mom and Ezra. He promised to kill them if I didn't go to him. I couldn't let that happen. I ran."

And she'd been running ever since.

She tipped her face up and he carefully wiped away her tears.

"No more running," Hunt murmured.

She bit her lip.

"Promise me, Savannah. *Trust* me. We can stop him, and give you your life back."

She closed her eyes. "I want to believe."

Hunt pressed his lips to her temple. "Believe."

He peppered kisses down her face. She made a needy sound, and then turned and pressed her lips to his.

"*Hunter.*" She slid her hands into his hair. Their tongues stroked.

Fuck, she tasted so damn intoxicating. She moved on him, setting his already-hard cock throbbing. He gripped her thigh. "Savannah—"

"I want you. I want you inside me, filling me up."

Hunt groaned. This was pure torture. "I'm not fucking you tonight."

She frowned. "Why not? I want you. You want me."

"You've had a rough day and night."

"Hunt—"

He squeezed her hand. "Hear me out." He slid his fingers along her jaw. "You're tough. I know that. But you've dealt with a lot of stuff tonight. I'm not taking advantage of that. When I finally have you, we'll both be focused solely on that."

She wrinkled her nose. "Guess it's my own fault for lusting after a slightly uptight, do-gooder cop." She put her hand over his. "And a good guy."

"If you knew exactly what I wanted to do to you, you might not say that."

She shivered.

"The other reason is, I don't have any condoms, and I'm guessing you don't, either."

"You don't?" There was surprise in her voice.

"Haven't needed any lately. I've had no time to date." He ran his thumb over her lips. "And no one caught my eye, until my annoying, sexy, new neighbor played her music too loud."

She nipped the end of his thumb, and Hunt felt it deep, his gut tightening.

"Well, we could do other stuff," she murmured.

"Savannah—"

She sucked his thumb into her mouth, gray gaze locked on his. "Please, Hunter? I want to pleasure you, feel connected to you. I want to touch you."

Fuck.

He felt his control crumbling. She bit his thumb again, giving him ideas of exactly what she wanted to do.

When he didn't respond, she smiled.

Her hand slid down between them, and she palmed his erection.

He groaned. "I feel like I should say no."

"Don't say no." She fumbled with the waistband of his shorts, then shoved them down. "I want—"

His large cock sprang free.

She stared. Hunt tried to think, but his brain was scrambled. He loved seeing the absorbed look on her face. "Baby, I—"

She dropped to her knees between his thighs, and leaned forward and licked the head of his cock.

He bit back a strangled curse and curled a hand in her curls.

She looked up, a faint smile on her face. "You were saying?"

"Nothing." He nudged her.

Her smile widened, then she sucked him deep. She licked, sucked, and found the perfect suction.

Hunt groaned and kept his gaze on her. On that pretty mouth stretched around his cock, and on the hunger written all over her face.

She made a sound, and the vibration on his cock was almost too much. His climax was drawing closer, and he felt everything in him tightening. She kept bobbing her head up and down, and Hunt was incapable of talking, could only manage wordless grunts.

She squirmed between his thighs, drawing back, then taking him deep.

"Savannah, baby, I'm going to come." His fingers tightened in her hair.

She sucked him deeper.

Hunt shuddered, throwing his head back. Hot, molten pleasure rushed through him. He shot into her mouth, and she swallowed, her hands digging into his thighs.

Shit. *Fuck.*

His body was a mass of pleasure, relief, and violent satisfaction.

She smiled up at him, her face open and flushed. Then he noted the way she rubbed her thighs together.

He didn't stop to think or warn her.

He yanked her up, then tossed her on the couch.

"*Hunter—*" Her voice was breathless.

"Quiet." He yanked her shorts and panties off. He pushed her legs apart, spreading her wide. He was desperate for a taste of her.

He kissed her thigh, scraped his teeth over the delicate skin. She shuddered.

Then he put his mouth on her pretty pussy.

She reared up. With long swipes of his tongue, he explored and tasted. He groaned, using his tongue to torment her. She let out a sharp cry.

Hunt found her clit. He scraped it with his teeth, and sucked.

She turned her head into the couch cushion and screamed as she came.

He felt pleasure ripple through her before she collapsed under him, panting.

Yes, Savannah Cole was his.

He wouldn't let her stalker have her, wouldn't let her run from him, and he'd fight anyone who tried to hurt her or take her away.

CHAPTER TEN

Savannah whistled in the shower.

Why the hell not?

She smiled as she washed her hair. She'd had the best orgasm of her life, made even better because it wasn't self-induced. She'd gotten to touch and taste Hunter, and give him pleasure.

She'd slept tucked up against Hunt's hard body. The man liked full contact when they slept. He'd kept his body pressed to hers, an arm tight around her waist.

After shutting off the water, she stepped out. She dried her hair and wrapped herself in a towel. Despite the shitty circumstances of her life and the ugly bruises around her neck, she felt good. She was going to enjoy the moment.

Movement in the mirror caught her eye. Hunt stepped into the bathroom. He'd already dressed in dark suit pants, a white shirt, and tie.

Mmm. She absorbed the shot of desire. She wanted to mess the detective up a little.

He set the coffee mug down on the vanity, then snaked an arm around her and kissed her.

Oh. She clung to him. He tasted like coffee and Hunt.

He bit her bottom lip. "If we had time, I'd get rid of this towel, and bend you over the vanity until you scream."

She groaned. "Seriously, you're hot enough without the sexy, dirty talk."

He smiled at her, then squeezed her ass through the towel. "I remember exactly how sweet you taste. Unfortunately, I have meetings, and I need to get you to Norcross."

"Norcross?"

He nodded. "Vander's going to keep an eye on you today. Take your art stuff. You can work at his office."

She hated the idea that she needed bodyguards, but if she was safe, she knew that Hunt would be less distracted and could focus on finding Walkson.

"Here." Hunt handed her the coffee.

She sipped her coffee and moaned. "Careful, I could get used to this."

He met her gaze in the mirror. "Good."

Then he was gone.

Her chest tightened to a hard, sharp point. She wanted this. Wanted this happiness to last. She pressed a hand to the sink, and her chin dropped to her chest. She knew life could kick you in the teeth and snatch everything you loved most away in the blink of an eye.

She looked into the mirror.

No. She'd told Hunt that she'd stay, and that they'd face Walkson together.

She dressed in fitted, three-quarter, navy-blue pants, some beaded, flat sandals, and her favorite gray T-shirt. She put on the black choker necklace she loved, and it covered the bruising a little. She piled her loose curls up on top of her head.

Hunt herded her and her art bag into his now working Charger. They prowled out of the neighborhood.

"Busy day?" she asked.

"Hell, yeah. I'm juggling a bunch of cases. I just got a message that there's been a follow-up on one, so I need to chase that down. We might finally arrest the perp responsible today."

"You love your job."

He glanced at her. "Sometimes. It has its ups and downs. It helps to know I'm making a difference. That I'm there when it counts."

There was something in his voice.

There when it counts. Her belly clenched. Like he felt he hadn't been for his Delta Force men.

"Hunt, being a cop, it's important. You don't need to be making up for the Delta brothers you lost."

"It's not that," he snapped.

Savannah watched his hands flex on the wheel, his knuckles white. She felt a funny sensation. "I can't bring Amelia back."

He growled. "Her death is *not* your fault."

"And neither were the deaths of your friends after you left the military."

"Drop it."

"Hunt—"

"I said, drop it."

She folded her arms. "Right, I bare all my secrets, but yours are off-limits."

He was silent, a muscle in his jaw ticked.

She felt a sense of sadness. She looked out the side window. "Maybe I'm just another case for you to solve. Another person for you to save as you make amends for your lost friends."

"*No.*" He blew out a breath. Then he yanked on the wheel and pulled over on a side street.

He reached out and took her hand.

"I'm sorry. I... Haven't talked about Eric, Mitchell, and Manny much."

"Oh." He'd never shared with anyone?

"I talk a little bit with Ryder. I do feel guilt. Survivor guilt. I know it. Those men all had families, kids, and Manny had a baby on the way. I was single. Maybe a part of me thought it would be better if I had died."

"Hunter, no." She touched his cheek. "Life sucks sometimes. Sometimes there is no good explanation for why things happen. You just have to accept them and move on."

He kissed her, thorough but quick. "I'll try not to snap your head off in the future."

"That'll be appreciated, but I do get it, Hunt."

He kissed her hand, then pulled the car back out onto the road.

It wasn't long before he pulled up in front of an amazing, renovated warehouse. *Wow.* A large door slid open, and they drove into the parking area. Rows of BMW SUVs were parked on one side.

"Nice digs."

"Private security pays well," Hunt said. "And Vander's brother is a billionaire."

"Wait. Easton Norcross?"

"That's him. He helps us all invest."

She knew that the billionaire owned the Hutton Museum. It was one of her favorite places to visit in San Francisco. The art collections there were amazing.

"Really? Are you loaded, Detective?" She bumped her hip against his as he slung her art bag on his shoulder.

"Well, I'm not a billionaire." He led her up some stairs.

No, he wouldn't want billions. "Bummer. Can you introduce me to Easton?"

Hunt gripped the back of her neck. "Sure, but he's happily engaged."

She wrinkled her nose. No doubt Easton Norcross was engaged to some statuesque supermodel.

Hunt nipped Savannah's ear. "And you're mine."

She shivered.

They reached the top of the stairs, and Savannah stopped to take it all in. She totally loved the industrial feel to the warehouse interior. Whoever had done the work, had done an excellent job.

The next thing she spotted was a tall, golden-haired man in a tailored suit, kissing a petite, dark-haired woman in a sleek, blue dress that Savannah instantly coveted.

The man lifted his head, saw Hunt and smiled.

"Can't stay away from your woman, Buchanan?" Hunt asked.

The man slung his arm across the woman's shoulders. "Why would I want to stay away? She's gorgeous, mine, and going to marry me."

"She's going to smack you if you don't let her leave. I have a meeting, and Ashley will skin me alive if I'm late. Sometimes I wonder who's the boss and who's the assistant." The brunette eyed Savannah with interest. "Hi, I'm Gia Norcross. This is my man, Saxon Buchanan."

"Savannah."

"Vander's taking care of Savannah for me," Hunt said. "She's got some troubles."

Gia's gaze flickered briefly to the bruises on Savannah's neck. "Bodyguard duty." There was sympathy in the woman's voice.

A slightly disheveled brunette in a fitted, green pantsuit stepped out of an office. "Rhys, I have to go."

A far-too-hot-for-his-own-good man stepped out behind her. He looked like a rock god crossed with a fallen angel. He had a handsome face, thick, dark hair with curl to it, and a wide smile.

Oh, Savannah wanted to paint him, bare chested, guitar in hand.

"Oh, hello." The woman blushed prettily, especially when the man kissed the back of her neck.

"Rhys Norcross and Haven McKinney, this is Savannah Cole," Hunt introduced her.

"It's lovely to meet you," Haven said.

"Actually, I've been meaning to introduce you two," Hunt added. "Savannah's an artist."

Haven's face perked up. "Really? I'd love to see your work."

"Well, sure," Savannah said.

"Haven works at the Hutton Museum," Hunt said.

Savannah gasped. "I *love* the Hutton. I've spent hours there. The Carolina Exhibition is amazing."

Haven beamed. "I spent hours securing that collection. I'm the curator."

Brynn and Vander strode down the hall, and Savannah took a second to admire them. They had a similar, take-charge vibe. A matching set. Then Vander pulled Brynn close, he ran his nose down hers, and watched her intensely the entire time. Savannah felt like a voyeur. *Phew*. They sure generated some heat.

Vander lifted a hand to the crowd.

"Hi, Savannah," Brynn said

"Hi."

Gia frowned. "So, Savannah, do you know Hunt from a case?"

"Sort of..."

"She's my neighbor," Hunt said.

"Oh," Gia said.

"I need to go," Hunt said. "Stay inside, follow Vander's orders."

Savannah nodded.

"So, there's nothing going on with you two?" Gia asked, not even bothering to hide her nosiness. The woman had a look in her eye.

"I have a stalker," Savannah said.

"That's terrible," Haven said. "I'm so sorry."

"But there's also plenty going on." Hunt tugged Savannah close and laid a kiss on her.

When he finally stepped back, her head was swimming, and her girly parts were doing the rumba.

She looked up. The men all looked amused, and the women were eyeing her with wide grins.

"I'll pick you up this afternoon," he said.

She watched him stride to the stairs.

Damn the man.

IT WAS a little surprising to find herself in a beautiful, light-filled space, showing her sketchbook to Haven.

"Oh, look at Hunt in this. That man has hot, dependable, cop written all over him." Haven smiled at Savannah. "But don't worry, I like hot, sexy, rock-star investigators myself." She looked down at the sketchbook. "Your style is amazing."

"I paint and sculpt, too."

Haven's blue eyes lit up. "Can I see?"

Savannah nodded. "I actually had some showings, before..."

Haven grabbed her hand and squeezed. "When I got together with Rhys, I found myself in some trouble. There was a theft at the Hutton, and a Monet was stolen."

Savannah's mouth dropped open. "I heard about that in the news."

"I was there. It was horrible. It turned out my ex,

who'd hit me, was involved. Anyway, I have no idea how it feels to have a crazed stalker after you, but I do know how it feels to have your life spin out of control, and to be afraid. I also know how difficult it can be to trust a gorgeous man who wants to help you."

Savannah felt a sense of kinship and understanding. Smiling, she pulled out her phone. "I've got some pictures of my paintings. It's not the same, of course, but..."

She showed Haven and the woman squeed. "*Amazing*. Your painting style is incredible. Oh, my God, you've had to hide this?" Haven straightened. "Once Hunt has your stalker locked up, you're having a showing at the museum."

Savannah froze, certain her hearing was suddenly failing. "Wait, what? At the Hutton?"

"Yes. I'm going to make it happen."

Savannah blinked. "Haven, I..." She didn't know what to say. She hadn't been safe for so long. Hadn't been in a position where she could actively plan for the future.

Haven hugged her, and Savannah's throat tightened. She hadn't spoken to her best friend, Saskia, since she'd been on the run.

Savannah missed her so much—the camaraderie, someone to confide in, joke with.

"Trust the good," Haven said. "Grab him with both hands and hold on."

Savannah smiled. "You're right. Thank you, Haven. Oh my God, my art in the Hutton."

Vander appeared, striding down the row of glass-walled offices. Something about him made her think of a stalking panther. Then she saw his face and the bottom of her stomach dropped away.

"Something's wrong." A rock lodged in her throat. "What happened?"

Vander put his hands on his hips, his face grim. "Hunt's been shot."

The world blurred around her. Noise roared in her ears.

Haven grabbed her hand and squeezed hard.

"Is he—?" Savannah's voice broke. "Is he okay?"

God. *God.*

"He's on the way to the hospital."

"Was it a criminal?" Haven asked. "Were cops targeted?"

Vander's lips flattened. "He was shot at a crime scene by a long-range sniper rifle."

Savannah tasted bile. "It's Walkson." This was all her fault. She should have left. She'd known Walkson would target Hunt. "This is my fault."

"No, it's not," Vander bit out. "Hunt will be fine. He's a tough sonofabitch, and one of the best Delta soldiers I ever worked with. He's going to be pissed, and I'm feeling pissed, myself. This asshole doesn't get to hurt you, or my friends, or terrorize my city."

Vander's cold, lethal tone made Savannah's chest lock.

"I'll take you to the hospital." Then Vander closed the distance between them and cupped her cheek. "You're safe, Savannah. Walkson's reign of fucking terror is over. I'll do everything I can to help Hunt take the fucker down."

"Thanks, Vander," she murmured.

"Let's go."

Haven hugged her, then Vander bundled her into a black BMW X6.

The drive to the hospital was a blur. Her heart beat hard in her ears. Hunt could've died. He could still die. How badly was he hurt? She twisted her hands together in her lap. Terror carved up her insides.

"Did you tell his brothers?" she asked.

"I called them. Camden was out on a job for me, but he'll meet us at the hospital."

"Walkson is sneaky. He never comes head-on, and he likes being cunning, and conning everybody."

"He's done. I'll either see him dead, or locked up."

She eyed him curiously. "Hunt must give you the 'you can't do that because I'm a detective' speech pretty often?"

The corner of Vander's lips twitched. "All the time. I bribe him with bourbon."

"Blanton Gold."

"That, and sometimes a bottle of George T. Stagg."

"Sounds expensive."

"It costs about twelve hundred dollars a bottle."

She choked. "Jesus."

Vander smiled. "Don't ask Easton about his collection. Hunt secretly covets the Stagg, but anything too expensive makes him twitchy." Vander's hands flexed. "He'll be fine."

Savannah prayed that that was true.

Vander pulled in at the hospital. He kept her close to

his side, his dark gaze scanning everyone who passed them as they headed into the building.

He talked to someone at the nurses' desk, but Savannah still couldn't focus. He led her into a private waiting room.

A small crowd had gathered.

There were several cops, many in uniform, but some in suits. Brynn hurried over and hugged Vander, lines of worry digging into her face. Then she let Vander go and hugged Savannah.

Savannah quickly got over her surprise and clung to the woman.

"He will be *fine*," Brynn said. "I know it."

Savannah wished she felt so confident.

Ryder and Cam appeared, both radiating deadly intensity.

"He was shot in the arm," Cam said. "Bastard who shot him was aiming for his chest, but Hunt moved at the last minute."

Savannah gasped, and locked her shaky knees.

Ryder slung an arm over her shoulders. "He'll be all right. That last mission, his knee was a mess, and he walked for miles and carried out an injured teammate."

"That sounds like Hunt," she said.

The door burst open, and a tall, older woman with carefully dyed, ash-blonde hair hurried in.

She spotted Ryder and Cam, and hurried to them.

"Mom." Camden caught the woman.

There were tears in her eyes and she fought them back. "How is he?"

"No news yet." Ryder said. "Other than we know he got hit in the arm, and he's conscious."

Mrs. Morgan blew out a breath. "Okay, that doesn't sound too bad." Then her gaze fell on Savannah and she fought not to fidget.

"Ryder, are you seeing someone and didn't tell me?" There was a hopeful note in the woman's voice.

Despite the circumstances, Ryder grinned. "As much as I'd like to say yes, Savannah's not mine. She belongs to Hunt."

Mrs. Morgan's eyes—the same green that she'd given her sons—widened. "Oh." Her smile bloomed. "I'm Delia. It's a pleasure to meet you." She stepped forward and hugged Savannah.

"You, too. I'm so sorry about Hunter."

"Hunter. You call him Hunter." Mrs. Morgan stared at her for a beat, then waved a hand. "It's not your fault. Hunt will catch whoever did this, and Vander will help." Her voice was matter-of-fact.

Vander inclined his head.

"I think it's my fault," Savannah confessed. "I have a stalker, and I think he did this."

Mrs. Morgan squeezed Savannah's hand, her gaze dropping to Savannah's bruised neck, and something sparked in her eyes. "That doesn't make it your fault."

The internal doors opened, and a young, male doctor in blue scrubs entered. "Hunter Morgan?"

Everyone in the room turned.

"Ah, his family?" the doctor added.

Ryder and Cam moved, and Mrs. Morgan grabbed Savannah's hand and yanked her forward.

"How's my son?" Mrs. Morgan asked.

"He's stable. The gunshot cut across his arm, and there's no permanent damage. He's lucky."

"He's okay," Ryder announced to the room.

The cops broke out in cheers.

"Can we see him?" Mrs. Morgan asked.

"Family only, for now," the doctor said.

"Come on." Hunt's mom kept a tight grip on Savannah.

"Mrs. Morgan, I—"

Cam took her other arm. Ryder nudged her back.

"Let's move, beautiful," the paramedic said.

CHAPTER ELEVEN

Hunt shifted on the bed, fighting off his annoyance. The nurse checked his vitals, then fussed with the bandage on his arm.

"I think it's good." He did his best to temper his voice. He'd been shot before; more than once, in fact.

Savannah would panic. Again, she'd get it in her head that she had to protect him and try to run. His pulse spiked. What if she slipped away?

Vander had her. No one could slip past Vander.

"You need to rest, Detective," the nurse said. "And take your pain meds."

He knew the drill. He was just glad he hadn't needed surgery.

The door opened. His mom led the charge, but Hunt's gaze went straight to Savannah. She was wedged between his brothers, her face pale, and her lips pressed tightly together.

Hunt swung his legs over the bed.

"Detective," the nurse squawked.

He took two steps and yanked Savannah into his arms. "You aren't leaving, and this is *not* your fault."

"Hunter..." A near soundless whisper. Then her arms wrapped around him and held tight.

That was better. He looked over her head. "Hi, Mom."

"Hunt." She leaned close and touched his cheek. Her worried look melted away as she watched him and Savannah. A smile touched her lips.

Delia Morgan had been a cop's wife. She'd had three sons in the military. She was made of sturdy stuff.

Even after she'd lost her husband to a stroke, she'd never faltered. His mom was like a rock. The foundation of their family.

She'd always supported whatever decisions they made about their careers, and never pushed them to marry or have kids. But the look in her eye warned him that she'd been thinking about it.

"I'm about to be discharged," he told them. "I'm fine."

Savannah lifted her head and eyed the bandage on his arm with unhappy eyes.

He cupped her chin. "I'm *fine*. This is good. The asshole hired someone to take the shot."

Savannah gasped.

"We got the guy. He's singing like a canary, and he described Walkson as the man who hired him."

Savannah's hands flexed on Hunt's skin.

"We've confirmed he's in San Francisco," Hunt continued. "I also made contact with the NYPD."

She tensed.

"You aren't the suspect from Amelia's murder, Savannah. You were only ever a person of interest. I know the questioning made you feel that way, but people lie a lot, and thorough questioning is vital."

She nodded. "I don't care about any of that right now. Walkson's after you."

Hunt slid his hand into her hair. "Good. He'll get sloppy."

"He's already hurt you..."

Fear coated her voice. He hated it, but he knew that it showed she felt something for him.

That made him feel good.

There was a knock at the door and Vander appeared in the doorway. "You done lying around, Morgan?"

Hunt snorted.

"It's too dangerous for you to go home," Vander said. "Walkson knows where you live, Hunt. Today, he proved he's willing to resort to any tactics."

Hunt frowned. *Shit*. That was all true.

"And you can't stay with your family or friends either," Vander added. "That'll just put them in danger."

Savannah's fingers tightened on him.

"I think Sunday lunch is off," Hunt said to his mom.

His mom waved a hand. "I just want you and Savannah safe."

Vander continued, "I spoke with Easton, and we've organized a safe house for you and Savannah. Somewhere safe, comfortable, and well protected. I'll have my team supplement security." Vander's face hardened. "And then we can make a plan to track this fucker down." His gaze flicked to Hunt's mom. "Sorry, Mrs. Morgan."

The older woman smiled. "I've heard the word before, Vander. In fact, I've heard you and my boys use it quite a few times."

Vander gave her a faint smile.

"And I want you, Hunt, and my boys to catch the fucker," she said.

"Mom," Ryder said, grinning.

Savannah laughed. Hunt squeezed her closer.

"I'll drop you at the safe house," Vander said. "Cam can get clothes and whatever else you need from your place."

"Savannah will need her art gear," Hunt said.

"Oh, you're an artist." Hunt's mother clapped her hands together. "That's wonderful."

"Okay, let's spring Hunt, and get these two safe," Ryder said.

Hunt met Vander's gaze. "We need to find Walkson. Fast."

Vander nodded. "Rhys and Ace are on it. We'll run him down."

Savannah stiffened, and Hunt stroked her back.

Once the paperwork was done, Hunt's mom kissed him and Savannah, then headed off with Ryder.

Vander herded them into the back of his X6.

"You're sure you're all right?" She stroked his fingers.

"Fine." The bandage poked out of the borrowed scrub shirt he wore. "It cut a groove in my bicep, but there's no bad damage. The painkillers are controlling the pain."

She looked unhappy, and he gave her a quick kiss.

Hunt made a quick call and spoke with his lieutenant. Lieutenant William Cook was smart, fair, and solid. Hunt liked working for him.

"Lay low, Hunt, and find this Walkson," Lieutenant Cook rumbled. "Whatever resources you need, you have them. No one gets away with taking potshots at cops in my city."

"Yes, sir. I'll keep you updated."

It wasn't long before Vander drove past the main entrance to the Four Seasons and pulled into one of the private residence towers around the corner.

"Exactly where is the safe house?" Savannah asked.

Vander turned and looked back at them. "It's more of a safe apartment. Easton owns a slew of properties across the city. This one's in the residential tower here, on a high level, and the building has an excellent security system."

"Installed by Norcross Security?" Hunt asked.

"Of course. The building has a good security team too, plus I'll have my team beef that up, and control access to your floor."

They strode to a private elevator. Vander pulled out a key card and held it to the panel. As the elevator zoomed upward, he handed the card to Hunt.

"You'll be safe here. Tomorrow, Ace, Rhys and I will come by with whatever we have on Walkson. We can make a plan of attack."

"You guys are doing so much..." Savannah fiddled with her hair. "All because of me."

"Because you deserve to be safe," Hunt said.

"Because Walkson has to be stopped before he hurts anyone else."

The elevator slowed and the doors opened. They walked into the apartment.

Hell. Hunt couldn't think of anything to say.

Savannah's mouth dropped open. "Holy cow. Vander, you should've said safe *penthouse*."

The space was flooded with natural light. There was a double-height living area, with huge, floor-to-ceiling windows. Savannah looked dumbfounded, and Hunt was a little in awe himself.

Sleek, gray couches were grouped around a flat, black coffee table. The windows in front of them gave breathtaking views of the city and the Bay. To the left, a half spiral staircase led up to the mezzanine level and upper floor. Beyond that, were more windows that showed off the Salesforce building and rest of the city. Sliding doors opened onto a terrace, with outdoor furniture and a long, infinity pool.

To the right was the dining room with a huge table and another terrace.

"Kitchen's stocked," Vander said. "Get some rest, Hunt, then be ready to hunt Walkson down."

"Bye, Vander," Savannah said. "Please thank your brother for letting us stay here."

Once Vander was gone, Savannah strode over to Hunt.

"You need to rest." Her tone turned bossy. "I'll make you something to eat and—"

"Don't fuss."

She huffed out a breath. "I'm going to fuss. I'm freaked, worried, and you got *shot*." Her voice rose. She was wired, tense.

"I don't need you to fuss."

She met his gaze. "What do you need?"

"You." He tilted her head up. "I'm going to have you now, Savannah."

INSTANT DESIRE.

Heat pooled in her belly. It really didn't take much with this man. Hunt just had to be in the room, and she was wet. She tried to find some control.

"Your arm—"

"Is fine. How many more times are you going to make me say that?" He kissed her. His hand cupped the back of her head, tongue stroking into her mouth.

She moaned, kissing him back.

His other hand gripped her ass. He pulled her flush against him, his big, hard cock pressing against her belly.

God. She wanted his cock inside her. Wanted to feel the flex of his muscles as he thrust into her.

"You're sure?" she asked. "I don't want you in pain."

"I'm sure." He covered her mouth with his again and backed her up.

"*Please*," she said.

"Please, what?" His voice was deep, guttural.

"Please fuck me."

He growled, then gripped her waist and lifted her effortlessly onto the long, shiny dining table.

Savannah glanced over her shoulder. The windows gave amazing views of the city. Then she felt Hunt working to open her pants, and all she saw was the stark, hungry need on his rugged face.

She gripped his arms, narrowly avoiding his gunshot wound.

Oh, boy. She loved his strong arms. Her fingers traced over the ink on his forearm. It was intricate and a fascinating piece of art. It looked like a kraken—wild and powerful—with its tentacles wrapped around his muscular arm. There was writing as well, but she didn't get a chance to read it.

Hunt yanked her pants free, then his mouth was back on hers.

The next kiss was hard and hungry. There was no gentleness or wooing—just a possessive claim, and pure need.

She pressed into him, frantic for more. She felt like she'd waited her entire life for this man.

He pushed her legs apart. His fingers stroked over her lace panties.

"I need to taste that sweet pussy again," he growled.

Her belly contracted. He gripped her panties, then, with a flick of his wrist, tore them off her.

She gasped, pulling his head back to hers. Their tongues clashed, as his fingers stroked between her legs.

Then he broke the kiss, and dropped to his knees.

Oh God. *Oh God.*

His big hands spread her farther, then his mouth was on her.

Oh.

Savannah clamped her hands on his head. Her legs spasmed, and Hunt gripped her thighs, and pulled her hard against his marauding mouth.

His tongue licked and stabbed, and Savannah's cries bounced off the windows. She tugged on his hair. "Hunt. I need you inside me. Now!"

He surged up. She attacked his scrub shirt, shoving it up. He ripped it over his head.

She leaned forward and kissed his chest. She made a promise to herself to take the time to explore every inch of him. *Later*.

With a short grunt, he opened his pants and freed his straining cock.

Oh, yes. The head of him was leaking with need. He pulled something from his pocket and ripped the condom package open.

Clearly, he'd sorted out the condom problem. Belly tight and hot, she watched him roll the latex on his thick cock.

Then he looked up.

The heat and hunger in his green eyes made her chest hitch.

Hunt pulled her to the edge of the table, and she tucked her legs tight to his sides. His thick cock brushed her damp folds, making her gasp.

Then he thrust inside her.

"*Hunter*." She threw her head back, wrapping her arms tightly around him.

He groaned against her neck. "Right where I needed to be."

He pulled back, then drove deep. He started a hard, powering rhythm.

He felt *so* good inside her. He felt so right. She clung to him as he thrust into her.

"Tight. Perfect." He groaned. "You fit me just right, baby."

"I'm going to come," she panted.

"Good. I can't wait to feel you clench down on my cock."

Pleasure—hot and violent—hit her, washing over her in waves. She screamed his name, drowning in ecstasy. She gripped him tight as he thrust deep and found his own release. His big body shuddered over hers.

She pressed her face against his neck. She couldn't think, let alone speak.

Breathing heavily, Hunt lifted his head. Their gazes met, electric, then he looked down.

"Fuck, baby, I love seeing how you take me." He stroked where she was stretched around his still-hard cock. Her body jolted.

A smile tilted his lips as he pulled out.

She moaned at the sensation, fighting the sense of loss.

He took a second to deal with the condom, tossing it in the trashcan near the sideboard. Then he was back. Clearly, he didn't care that he was naked.

"I hope no one has a telescope." She nodded at the windows.

Hunt smiled. "I bet they'd enjoy the show. It's unlikely they can see through these windows, though. They're treated with a privacy film."

"Handy." She reached out and touched two puckered scars on his chest. She gently ran her fingers over them.

"Took two bullets," he said. "Afghanistan."

She leaned forward and kissed them. She hated the idea that he'd been hurt, could've died.

"This one's from a knife wound." He pointed to his side.

It was a jagged scar and she caressed it gently.

"Knee's a mess. Had a bunch of surgeries."

He shifted his leg and she saw his left knee was covered in scar tissue.

He met her gaze, then gripped the hem of her T-shirt and pushed it up.

Panic flooded like butterflies in her belly.

No. This was Hunt. She was safe, and he'd just fucked her brains out. He clearly liked her, even if she had a few scars.

He bared her belly. She felt like the long, silvery scars were so glaring in the light. She swallowed.

Hunt bent over and kissed them.

As his mouth traced each one, she was shocked as her desire rekindled.

He took his time before he lifted his head. "You're fucking beautiful, Savannah."

Then he scooped her up and tossed her over his shoulder.

"Hunter!"

He smacked her butt lightly.

"Your arm," she said.

"Is still fine."

"Put me down."

"No." He strode through the magnificent living area.

"What about your knee?" she tried.

"That's fine, too." He started up the spiral stairs. "I'm not putting you down. I want you spread under me on the bed, next. And I'm warning you, Savannah, that's just for starters."

CHAPTER TWELVE

Hunt woke, his arm throbbing.

Wincing, he sat up, and checked his bandaged wound. He'd need some more pills soon to combat the ache.

The bed was wrecked. He'd barely paid any attention to the luxurious room done in soothing, pale grays and blues. The sheet was covering half of one of his legs. There was no sign of Savannah.

He grabbed his phone, feeling a flicker of panic in his gut. He checked the security system. Nothing had been triggered, no doors opened, since Cam had stopped by the night before and dropped off their bags.

Hunt pulled on his shorts and stopped for a second. He'd gorged himself on Savannah last night. He'd barely let her sleep. After their first frenzied fuck on the dining table, he'd had her over and over.

Damn, the sounds she made, the look she got when he was moving inside her...

Even at the memories, his cock lengthened.

He wanted her again. She was a damn addiction; one he was happy to keep indulging. He grabbed a condom packet off the bedside table and slipped it into his pocket.

He strode out of the bedroom and descended the stairs to the living room. He saw her sketchbook and pencils on the coffee table. Bright, morning light streamed in the tall windows. Hunt took a second to admire the view of his city and the water.

He rarely took the time to enjoy San Francisco's offerings. Work kept him too busy.

And Savannah was right, it was easier to run from the guilt and keep too busy, than to face it. Maybe a part of him did bury himself in work as a way to make it up to his lost brothers in arms.

Maybe it was time to find some balance in his life?

He reached the bottom of the stairs. The doors to the main terrace were open, and he wandered out. Perfectly pruned trees in large pots lined the terrace, but his gaze went straight to the infinity pool... And the woman in it.

She rose up, her back to him, pushing her wet hair back from her face. The tiny strings at the back, between her shoulder blades, made him wonder what her bikini looked like.

Gut tight, he strode toward the pool.

Savannah turned and spied him. He loved the look on her face: a faint flush, a little shy, eyes filled with desire.

"Good morning," he said.

"Morning." She moved to the edge of the pool. "You were sleeping soundly, and I felt the urge to sketch."

"I would have liked to have woken up with you, but

this is nice, too." He strode to the steps of the pool and walked straight in.

She laughed. "Your shorts—"

"Will dry off. What color is that bikini, Ms. Cole?"

She watched him come toward her. "Does it matter?"

"It won't when it's in a wet pile beside the pool."

She licked her lips. "Do you have plans, Detective?"

"I do. Get my cock inside you."

She sucked in a breath.

"That okay with you?" he asked.

"Yes." Her voice was breathy.

He wrapped an arm around her and nipped her shoulder.

She slid her hand down his arm, her fingers tracing his ink. He'd noticed her checking it out before.

"I got it when I got accepted into Delta."

"It's a stunning bit of art." She cocked her head, reading the text. "Here be monsters."

"Old map makers used to write similar words on unknown portions of maps." He shrugged. "I knew I'd be headed into some unknown territory with my team. Plus, I loved reading John Steinbeck growing up. There was a quote from one of his books that stuck with me. 'Men really need sea-monsters in their personal oceans. An ocean without its unnamed monsters would be like a completely dreamless sleep.'"

"You were going to face the monsters," she murmured.

"Yes." He nipped her lips. "We all face our demons." He trailed his lips down her neck. "Now, enough talking, more pleasure."

"Can people see us?" she murmured.

Hunt swam them to the end of the pool, which was more private, and protected by a wall. He untied the strings on her small, red bikini top and freed her breasts. He made a hungry sound and pressed his mouth to one nipple.

She moaned and arched. He lavished her perfect breast with attention before moving on to the other one. She wrapped her legs around his waist, grinding against his erection.

Then he slid a hand down her belly, and into her tiny bikini bottoms. He stroked her.

"God, how can I want you this much?" she panted.

He kissed along her neck, while he worked the swollen folds between her legs. Her hips moved, the water splashing.

He spun her and pushed her forward until her upper body was flush against the paving around the pool. Her delectable ass was out of the water. Her breathing was fast.

He stroked his hands down her naked back. All that smooth skin. He kissed her between her shoulder blades. So beautiful.

He felt his calluses catch on her skin, but she was squirming, leaving no doubt how much she liked his touch. He moved lower, and untied the bikini bottoms, then stroked the globes of her ass, massaging them between his palms.

"Hunt—" She pushed back against his hands.

He leaned over her, rubbing his cock against her as he nipped her earlobe. "That's not what you call me."

"Hunter, stop teasing me."

He shoved his shorts off and dealt with the condom. Then he stroked her bottom again, before sliding two fingers into her slippery pussy. She let out a wordless cry.

He pulled his fingers free, desire a hard drumbeat in his head. Then he gripped her and pulled her back into the pool and onto his cock.

He plunged deep, filling her completely.

"Oh, oh... *Hunter*."

He wrapped an arm around her middle, using the water to help him move her. He stroked in and out, hot sensation pouring through him.

"God, you fill me up," she breathed.

Soon, Hunt couldn't think. He thrust wildly, moving his hand down to find her clit.

Savannah climaxed hard. She screamed, her body clamping down brutally on his cock.

He was thrusting with no finesse, his control gone. He plunged harder, faster, and his orgasm hit like an explosion.

"Fuck, Savannah." His body jerked as he poured himself inside her.

They stayed there in the water for a moment. She was boneless in his arms. He dropped a kiss to her shoulder, then spun her. She clung to him.

"It's a lovely morning," she mumbled.

Hunt laughed and carried her out of the pool. "It'll be even better after a shower and the breakfast I plan to make you."

"Pancakes?" she asked hopefully.

"That could be arranged." Shit, he realized that he'd

make pancakes, eggs, bacon, whatever she wanted, for this woman, every day for the rest of his life.

He sucked in a breath.

Getting ahead of yourself, Morgan. He had a stalker to deal with, first.

Then, an uncomfortable feeling filled his gut. After they dealt with Walkson, Savannah would get her life back. She'd be free, and could do anything she wanted, including go back to New York.

His gut locked.

For now, he'd keep her safe. Later, he'd convince her to stay.

They showered together and dressed. She sat on the kitchen counter, sketching, while he made pancakes.

Then she showed her great appreciation for his cooking, eating with gusto. Her smile made him feel like he'd won a million bucks.

"How's your arm?" she asked. "You shouldn't have gotten it wet in the pool."

"I didn't put it under the water. How's your neck?" The sight of those dark bruises made his gut churn.

"They're feeling a bit better, actually."

As he was cleaning up, his cell phone vibrated. He pulled it out of his pocket and read the message.

"Hunter?" There was worry in her voice. "Is everything okay?"

"Vander and Ace are on the way up. They have something."

She pressed a fist to the base of her throat, worry and tension leaking back in.

He slipped the phone in his pocket and pulled her to

his chest. He pressed a kiss to the top of her head. "It's going to be fine. You're terrible at this 'trusting other people' thing."

She hugged him back. "I'm out of practice."

They waited in the living room, Savannah pacing. The elevator chimed and her head jerked up.

Vander exited first, followed by Ace, then another man.

Hunt frowned. The guy was wearing an expensive, tailored, black suit. He had a sharp, handsome face, with ink-black hair, and black eyes. Those eyes were filled with piercing intelligence.

Suddenly, Savannah stiffened. Then she ran across the room. "Killian!"

She threw herself into the man's arms. The guy held her tight, his eyes closing for a second.

Hunt crossed his arms over his chest, battling a bunch of emotions that erupted all at once, and resisting the urge to yank her away from the man.

SAVANNAH HUGGED her best friend Saskia's brother.

She hadn't seen Killian since she'd left New York, but they'd emailed occasionally. It'd been Killian who had—against his own wishes—helped her run. He and his security company had helped put together her new identity.

"Damn, it's good to see you, Susannah," Killian said.

Killian Hawke looked like a sharp, lethal businessman, but he had a voice that made a woman blink. It always made her think of hot nights and melted chocolate.

"It's Savannah now, remember?" She wasn't sure she could be Susannah Hart again, even if Walkson was gone.

Killian touched her cheek. The man really was gorgeous, with his sharply defined features and piercing stare.

"I'm so glad you're okay," he said.

Suddenly, a hand gripped her hip and pulled her away from Killian. She bumped against Hunt's big body and he curled an arm around her chest.

She watched Vander's lips twitch, and Ace grin.

"We haven't met," Hunt said, tone clipped.

She looked up and saw his jaw was set in hard lines.

"Hunt, this is Killian Hawke. A friend from New York."

Killian and Hunt locked gazes, until Savannah frowned.

"Hey." She elbowed Hunt. "Do not go all caveman on me, Hunter Morgan."

His arm tightened.

Shaking her head, she went up on her toes and nipped the underside of his jaw. "Killian is my best friend Saskia's brother. He helped me escape. He put my Savannah Cole identity together."

Hunt's arm loosened a fraction.

"Killian Hawke," Killian said. "I own Sentinel Security in New York."

Hunt nodded. "I've heard good things about your outfit. Cybersecurity?"

"Mostly."

"Detective Hunter Morgan, SFPD." He reached around Savannah, not letting her go, and shook Killian's hand.

"My team picked up chatter about Savannah, and then I got word that someone had hacked our system, looking into Savannah's ID."

Ace grinned and buffed his nails on his shirt. "I didn't dig deep, since we know you."

Vander lifted his chin. "We've worked with Killian before. He knows Zane, Liam, and Mav."

The three names registered with Savannah. "Wait, you know the Billionaire Bachelors of New York?"

Vander smiled. "They aren't bachelors anymore. And yes, they're friends, and Norcross Security does work for them on occasion."

"Killian helped us out on a little job in New York," Ace said. "Hence why I didn't take a longer stroll through your system."

Killian snorted. "You couldn't have gotten any further, Oliveira." The man's dark eyes moved back to Savannah. "I called Vander and asked to be brought up to speed."

"You didn't have to come all this way." Savannah smiled. "But I'm glad you did. I want to hear all about how Saskia is."

A faint smile crossed Killian's face. Man, these guys were all cut from the same cloth. Heaven forbid they show too much emotion.

"I have some letters from her."

A shot of sadness hit Savannah. Her friend must have

been so hurt when Savannah disappeared without a word. "Oh, I..." Her words dried up.

Hunt pressed her face to his chest.

"There's a fresh pot of coffee in the kitchen," Hunt said. "Let's talk. But Savannah's right, you didn't have to come all this way. We've got her."

Killian eyed him. "I'm sure, if you want her free of Walkson once and for all, you'll take all the help you can get."

Hunt nodded. "I want Walkson behind bars."

Savannah squeezed Hunt's arm. "I'll get the coffee."

A little while later, Savannah found herself sitting beside Hunt at the dining room table, trying not to think about the things he'd done to her on it yesterday. She fidgeted in her chair. Thank God she'd given it a thorough cleaning after their sexy shenanigans.

Killian and Ace sat on the other side of the table, and Vander sat at the head. Ace had his laptop open, and a projection up on the wall.

"Walkson is definitely in San Francisco and targeting Savannah," Vander told Killian. "He took a shot at Hunt. Hired a sniper. A guy who's ex-Army, and likes hunting. The man sang after a few pointed questions."

Savannah's stomach roiled. She'd come so close to losing Hunt.

"Walkson's been hunting Savannah for four years," Killian said. "He came close to finding her a couple times early on."

"But luckily Killian warned me," she said. "And I got better at covering my tracks."

"He didn't have her new name until now," Killian said with a frown.

"How did he get it?" Hunt asked.

"No idea. Something definitely sent him to San Francisco."

Savannah wrapped her arms around herself. "So how do we find him?"

Ace leaned forward. "I'm running searches, hoping to catch him on CCTV."

"He's smart," Killian said. "High IQ, and thinks he's clever. He knows how to avoid facial recognition. He often uses disguises, and wears glasses that reflect back light, distorting any capture of his face."

"He just keeps coming." Savannah blew out a breath. "I never understood why he fixated on me. At first, he said he loved my art, but then..."

Hunt gripped the back of her neck and squeezed. "There's no rhyme or reason, baby. He's sick."

She dragged in a breath. Under the table, she put her hand on his thigh and he pressed his other hand over hers.

It was enough to steady her.

"Ace, I'll have my guy hook in with you," Killian said. "Hex is my best computer specialist."

"Hacker," Vander said dryly.

Killian smiled. "Yes. Walkson will be holed up close by. And he likes his creature comforts. He will be staying at a good hotel, and probably have a suite."

Ace nodded. "I'm on it."

Killian leaned forward, his hands steepled on the

table. "There's something else I haven't told you, Savannah."

Dread curdled in her belly. "Are my mom and brother okay?"

"They're fine." Killian blew out a breath. "You know I've kept tabs on you and Walkson, as best I could."

She nodded, and tangled her fingers with Hunt's under the table.

"In the cities where you've lived over the last four years, those times he almost caught you... Shit."

"Spit it out, Hawke," Hunt said.

"There were murders. Unsolved murders of young, female artists. They were found stabbed, and mutilated." Killian's eyes darkened. "They were all young and blonde."

The room seemed to tilt around Savannah. "*No.*"

"I'm sorry, Savannah. I have no proof, but I'm certain Walkson is responsible."

"Because he couldn't get to me," she whispered brokenly. "It's my fault."

"Savannah." Hunt shifted closer.

"*No.*" She jerked to her feet. "It's *my* fault. He followed me, I led him to those places, and he ended those women's lives." She stumbled back.

Hunt growled, and advanced on her. She backed up.

Her back hit the wall, and an angry male hit her front.

"Look at me," he demanded.

She met his green gaze.

"This is *not* on you. It's on Walkson. You're a victim. Every death is on *his* hands."

"Hunter..." She bit back a sob.

"We're going to stop him." Hunt yanked her into his arms. "This is *not* on you."

But it felt like it was. All those young women...

Tears fell and Savannah held on tight to Hunt.

CHAPTER THIRTEEN

Hunt saw Vander, Killian, and Ace out.

It was Saturday, but he still needed to get to work to check in on how their own search for Andrew Walkson was progressing.

With Norcross Security, Sentinel Security, and the SFPD searching for the man, there was no way the asshole could stay hidden forever.

Vander was going to send Rome Nash, his best bodyguard, over to stay with Savannah. But first, Hunt needed to take his woman's temperature. Make sure she was dealing with Killian's revelations.

If Walkson was responsible for a slew of murders of young women, then Hunt wouldn't mind seeing the man get the death penalty. Shame there was a moratorium on it.

He headed into the living room. Savannah was at the window, staring out at the city, her arms wrapped around herself.

He walked toward her.

"I'm okay," she said quickly.

"You're not."

She whirled. "All right, I'm not, but I'll get there. Eventually." Her eyes sparked. "That asshole!" She threw her arms up. "How dare he think he has the right to terrorize me, destroy my life, but even worse, to take the lives of innocent women. Amelia, all these girls that Killian mentioned—" her voice hitched "—I keep asking myself why. What could I have done differently to avoid this?"

"Nothing, baby." Hunt grabbed her arms. "Nothing. Bad people do bad things every day. Bad things happen every day. Unfortunately, they can happen to good people. You're entitled to be mad, and sad, and angry. I understand. I stood far from home, sweating in a godforsaken desert, dodging bullets, and saw good men die. At first, I would rage and try to find reasons so it made some sort of sense."

Now she wrapped her arms around him. *His sweet, giving Savannah.*

"But it makes no sense. It never will. So, we pick ourselves up, we deal the best way we can. If you wallow, it'll drag you down and swallow you whole."

"I'm sorry," she said.

"Don't be." He scooped her up and sat on the couch. "You're entitled to your feelings."

"But I'm only thinking of myself—"

"Again, in this situation, you're entitled."

She cupped his cheek. "I wasn't thinking of you. You've dealt with death and killers. You still do."

"I try to remember the people I help. The bad guys I lock away."

She snuggled into him, and he felt it in his chest. Damn, he liked that.

It was a sign that she was trusting him, and he knew the years had conditioned her to not trust anyone.

He ran a hand down her hair.

"You're going to catch Walkson," she said.

He met her gaze. "Yes, I am. Whatever it takes."

"I want to help. I *need* to help."

Hunt's muscles locked. The thought of her anywhere near Andrew Walkson made him revolt. "Savannah—"

She scrambled up. "Whatever I can do to help. I could help with searches."

"You can help by staying safe." He rose and pulled her around to face him.

"Hunter, I know him. I know how he works." She took a deep breath. "He wants me. You could use me as bait—"

"Absolutely not." Hunt gripped her arms. "There will be *no* baiting the stalker-slash-serial killer."

"I need to do *something*."

He stared into her pleading eyes and blew out a breath. *Dammit*.

"We'll work something out."

She beamed up at him, then went up on her toes and kissed him. "Thank you." Then she fidgeted a little.

He'd learned enough about her to know what that meant. "Need to sketch?"

She nodded.

"Get your sketchbook, baby. I need to change."

"Change?"

"I need to head to the station and follow up on some things."

She hissed out a sharp breath. "But you were *shot*. There's a madman after you."

"Vander's sending his best bodyguard, Rome, to stay with you."

She bit her lip.

Hunt hated seeing the fear in her eyes. "Rome's good, Savannah. He'll—"

"It's not that. Who's *your* bodyguard?"

Hunt's brows snapped together. "I'm a cop. I don't need a bodyguard."

"Walkson had you shot!" She spun away.

"Hey." He wrapped his arms around her from behind. "I'll take precautions. I know what I'm doing." Gently, he bit her earlobe.

She shuddered. "I don't want to lose you, Hunter."

"You won't." He kissed her neck.

She tilted her head to the side. "I don't want anyone else hurt."

"It's going to be fine." His phone chimed. With difficulty, he pulled himself away from her and checked it. "Rome's on his way up."

Savannah grabbed her sketchbook and nodded.

Hunt met Rome at the elevator. The bodyguard was big, broad, with brown skin, and deep-green eyes.

"Hunt."

"Rome." He shook the man's hand.

Rome Nash exuded a calm, watchful vibe that made him so good at his job.

"Thanks for coming. Savannah's a bit shaken up, but she's tough."

Rome lifted his chin. "I'll take care of her."

"How's your princess?"

Rome's smile flashed white. "Keeping me on my toes."

On a previous job, Rome had fallen in love with Princess Sofia of Caldova. Sofie had surprisingly slotted into the Norcross gang quickly and easily. The princess also didn't hide how much she loved her fiancé.

"Come and I'll introduce you to Savannah," Hunt said.

She was on her knees at the coffee table, sketching, her hand moving fast. She looked up, blinked. She was totally lost in her work already.

Then her gaze snagged on Rome and she blinked again.

"Can I sketch you?" Then she shook her head and stood. "Sorry, I'm still in the zone."

Rome smiled. "I'm Rome Nash."

She held out her hand. "Savannah."

"Listen to Rome, and stay out of trouble," Hunt said.

Her nose wrinkled. "Damn, and here I was thinking of running around the streets. You've crushed my plans."

Rome gave a low chuckle.

Hunt tapped her nose. "I like it when you're sassy." He kissed her, and made it long and thorough.

Savannah looked a little glassy eyed. "You should come with a warning label, Detective." Her face turned serious. "Be safe."

"I will. I promise. See you later."

SAVANNAH WAS SITTING on the floor in front of the living room windows. The late afternoon light was just right.

She'd sketched Rome—big, tall, stoic, gorgeous Rome. He'd been good company. He talked when she wanted to talk, and he stayed quiet when she got busy with her art.

She'd worked like crazy to keep herself distracted. She was working on a series of sketches of Hunter. She shaded in one image of him.

These were just for her.

She realized her neck was stiff and she stretched it. That's when she noticed Hunt sprawled on the couch, watching her.

She jolted. "How long have you been there?"

He smiled. "Not long. I like watching you work, especially when you're so caught up in it."

"I didn't even hear you arrive." She scanned around. "Where's Rome?"

"Gone. He said to say goodbye. Actually, he said goodbye, but you didn't hear him, and he didn't want to disturb you."

She rose. "I got super inspired and lost track of time."

He cocked his head. "I hope Rome wasn't the cause of the sudden burst of inspiration."

She grinned. "No. I did sketch him, looking every inch the hunky bodyguard."

Hunt frowned.

"But someone else left me very inspired." She held out her sketchbook.

He took it and flipped through the pages. She watched his rugged face freeze.

"I'm...naked. I never posed like *this*."

She bit her lip. "Don't worry. They're for my eyes only."

She leaned over. The image he was looking at showed him sprawled on the bed, naked and gorgeous. Like a big, satisfied lion.

In the next one, he was standing by the windows, naked, a glass of his beloved Blanton Gold in hand.

"I've never stood like this, either," he grumbled.

"Artistic license. I have a good memory." Especially when it came to all things Hunter Morgan.

The next image made him suck in a breath.

He was naked under the shower, side on, cock very obviously hard. She felt the burn of desire and pressed her thighs together.

"Look at the next one," she said.

He flipped the page. He was sprawled on the very couch where he sat now, naked again, powerful thighs spread and his thick cock in hand. As he stroked, he was looking straight ahead.

He dragged in a breath. "*No one* but you ever sees these."

She nodded. "Of course." She licked her lips, feeling desperate for him. "Although I could probably make a small fortune—"

He growled.

Savannah wanted him, she always did, but she also wanted to keep from thinking about everything.

Hunter was the perfect distraction.

"Want to help make my vision a reality, Detective?" she asked silkily.

His eyes narrowed and he tossed the sketchbook aside. "You want to see my cock, beautiful?"

Her chest hitched, and she felt a flood of dampness rush to her panties. "Yes."

He eyed her for a beat, then unbuckled his belt. Electric tingles washed over her. Her gaze stayed locked on him as he opened his pants, then freed his cock from his boxers.

She swallowed a moan. He was already hard.

He stroked lazily. "Now, I want you to take your shorts off."

Her skin was on fire, and she quickly flicked them open and kicked them down her legs.

"Panties next. Hand them to me."

The deep, authoritative tone made her shiver. She hooked her fingers in the side of her panties and pushed them down.

Then she nabbed them and handed them to him.

"They're already wet."

"Yes," she breathed.

He pulled a condom out of his pocket, and she squirmed a little as she watched him roll it on.

"Shirt off next," he ordered.

She yanked it off. She wasn't wearing a bra. She felt his gaze on her, her nipples pebbling. As she watched, he gave his cock another lazy stroke.

"Touch your sweet pussy, Savannah."

His voice was so gritty, and her belly was full of heat

and flutters. She slid a hand down her belly. His green gaze stayed glued to it. She stroked through the curls at the juncture of her thighs, then she let out a little gasp.

"That's it," he drawled. "Stroke yourself."

She did, feeling how wet she was. She moved up to her clit and let out a low moan.

Hunt cursed. "So damn beautiful. Look how hard you've made me, Savannah."

She stared blindly. He was pumping his cock and she thought he was the beautiful one.

"Come here," he growled. "I want you to straddle me."

She closed the distance between them and eagerly straddled his lap.

This man, this good, solid man, had seduced her. She trusted him with everything. She knew in her bones that he'd never let her down.

She felt his hard cock beneath her. She shifted her hips, trying to get it right where she needed it.

"Uh-uh." He squeezed her hip. "Not yet." He took her hand, the one she'd used to touch herself, and sucked her fingers into his mouth.

Oh, God. Her belly clenched hard. Then he pulled her closer, and sucked her nipple into his mouth.

"*Hunter.*" She slid her hands into his hair, holding him to her.

Savannah moaned. She was entirely pure sensation. He moved to the other side, his big hands cupping her breasts as he sucked on her nipple.

She writhed, and let out a garbled cry.

Hunt tore his mouth free. "Put me inside you, Savannah, then sink down on my cock."

God, she'd never liked bossy men before, but these sexy orders left her panting. She grabbed his thick cock and shifted until it caught in her folds.

She bit her lip, then lowered down.

They both groaned.

Needy, hungry, she rocked on him, savoring the way he stretched her. She lifted her hips, expelling a sharp breath, then sank back down.

As always, she felt like her desire went from simmer to inferno. She rode him faster.

"No." He gripped her hips.

She froze. "What?"

"Slower. I want to make love to you. We've been all fire and flash."

Her heart slammed against her ribs. He'd said the L word. Panic took flight. "I like flash and fire."

He moved her body up, then eased her slowly back down on his cock. She moaned.

"There's no rush, baby. I've got you. Just feel."

His gaze stayed locked on hers, and he urged her into a slow rhythm.

Heat coiled inside her. This was so much more, so intimate. They were so connected.

He slipped his hand down and thumbed her clit. She jerked, but he kept her moving, slowly bumping his hips into her, filling her deeply.

"Feel that?" he murmured. "That's you and me, baby."

"*Hunter.*" She moved a little quicker, and after another thrust, her hot, slow, strong orgasm hit her. She cried out his name.

Hunt pressed his mouth to hers. Kissing her, his body shuddered as they came together.

CHAPTER FOURTEEN

Hunt stayed sprawled on the couch, lazily stroking Savannah's back.

She pressed into him, her breath puffing against his neck.

He'd gotten up to deal with the condom, but settled back on the couch with her on top of him. He'd be happy to stay right here for hours.

"Hell of a welcome home," he said.

She laughed. "It wasn't bad." She kissed his neck. "Do you want me to cook tonight, or will we order something in?"

"Actually, we're going out."

She lifted her head. "Where?" A groove appeared in her brow.

"To a party."

"Hunter, correct me if I'm wrong, but I have a killer stalker after me, and by extension, so do you. That's why we're here, in this very luxurious safe house."

He kissed her nose. "Don't worry. It's a little party at

Easton Norcross' place. The man has brilliant security, plus pretty much all of Norcross Security will be there, as well as Hawke and my brothers. Added to that, a Norcross vehicle will escort us over there."

"Are you sure it's safe?"

He squeezed her hip. "I promise. Now, shower and dress in something party-ish."

"When are we due?"

"In thirty minutes."

She squeaked and leaped off him. "Only a man would tell a woman she has thirty minutes to get ready. Especially a woman with curls."

"Actually, it's less than that, since we have to drive there."

She threw up her arms.

With a chuckle, Hunt rose and caught her for a quick kiss. "Relax, if we're a little late, it'll be fine."

She sprinted, beautifully naked, up the stairs.

By the time he headed up, she was getting out of the shower. He showered and dressed in gray pants and a button-down, black shirt. He took a second to admire Savannah in her white, lacy underwear as she leaned close to the mirror, doing her makeup.

He eyed her ass.

"Don't even think about touching me, Morgan. We'll be late enough as it is."

He met her gaze in the mirror. "Later."

Her lips parted. "Later."

As he waited for her downstairs, he checked in with Brynn and Ace. There had been no sign of Walkson.

Hunt sighed and looked out the window. The sun

was setting, and lights were flickering on across San Francisco.

Where are you? You can't hide forever, you monster. I will hunt you down.

He heard the click of heels. He turned and almost swallowed his tongue.

Savannah was making her way down the spiral staircase. She wore a long, flowing dress. It was white, with brilliant splotches of color on it in vibrant red and deep green. It almost looked like someone had tossed paint on it. It looked summery and fresh. The neckline plunged low, almost to her navel, and the skirt had a slit up one thigh.

He watched her slim leg appear as she walked. She had sexy black heels on that had a strap around her ankle.

He wanted to fuck her in them later.

Her blonde curls were loose, falling over one shoulder. He couldn't tell what she'd done to her face, but she looked dewy. She wore no jewelry, which just added to her fresh, sexy allure.

"Hunter?"

"We could stay in."

She shook her head. "No way. I just rushed to get ready. We're going." She tossed her head back. "Besides, I'm not letting Walkson rule my life anymore."

"Damn right." Hunt held out his arm.

She slid hers through his.

"You look beautiful," he told her.

"And you look hot."

They headed down to the garage and Rhys met them. The investigator whistled.

"Savannah, if I wasn't totally in love with Haven..."

Hunt glared at the man.

Rhys' smile widened and he winked at her. "I'll follow you in the X6."

Hunt led Savannah over to a low-slung, red, sports car. Her mouth dropped open.

"A Ferrari? Are you on the take, Detective?"

He snorted and opened the door. "The Roma is from Vander's collection. He said we shouldn't drive my Charger."

"This is his idea of inconspicuous?" She slid inside and stroked the leather seat.

"I don't think Walkson will be looking for us in a Ferrari." Hunt circled to the driver's side and gave Rhys a salute. The other man slid behind the wheel of a X6.

Hunt started the Ferrari, listening to the throaty purr of the engine. Okay, he could get used to this.

They headed out, the X6 behind them.

"So where does Easton live?" she asked.

"Broadway Street in Pacific Heights. It's known as Billionaire's Row."

When he turned onto Broadway, they passed some impressive houses before reaching Easton's. The four-story, cream-stucco mansion sat on a spacious corner block.

"Holy moly," Savannah murmured.

They drove into the underground garage and parked between Easton's Aston Martin DBS and Saxon's Bentley Continental.

A security guard nodded at them. "Detective. Ms. Cole. You're to head straight up."

"Thank you," Hunt said.

They took an elevator up and soon stepped out into a circular landing area with an ornate staircase in the center. Through a large doorway was the murmur of conversation punctuated by laughter.

Savannah looked around, staring up at the ornate chandelier. "This place..."

"Easton's a great guy. His fiancée, Harlow, is lovely, as well."

Savannah nodded, but didn't look convinced. They entered the open plan kitchen and living area. The kitchen had a large, stone island, and top-of-the-line appliances. The living area had built-in shelves around a huge TV, fronted by an elegant gray couch. A wall of sliding doors opened onto a grassed area walled in by a tall, green hedge for privacy.

"Hunt!" A bombshell blonde raced over and hugged him.

"Hi, Harlow."

"And this must be Savannah." Harlow smiled and shook Savannah's hand.

"Um, hi," Savannah said.

"I'm Harlow. It's *so* great to meet you. I'm already itching to get you to paint Easton for me. Haven said your artwork is *incredible*. Do you do commissions?"

"I...haven't, but I could."

"As long as he has clothes on," Hunt murmured.

A man joined them. "Hello, Savannah, I'm Easton."

Easton looked like a slightly older, less hard version of Vander. His Italian-American heritage was obvious in his rugged face and black hair. He looked every inch the successful, billionaire businessman.

"I can sketch him." Savannah said, looking a little dazzled.

Harlow beamed. "Great. Come and meet everyone else." Harlow dragged Savannah off. She sent Hunt a slightly helpless look, but was smiling.

It would be good for her to be around decent people, to relax. After holding herself apart, and running, she deserved it.

"Beer or bourbon?" Easton asked.

"Beer's fine. Thanks for the penthouse."

"It's my pleasure," Easton said. "Savannah's beautiful."

"She is. Now, I just have to keep her safe."

In the kitchen, Easton handed him a bottle of beer. Across the room, near the open sliding doors to the large terrace, Killian and Vander were talking with Ryder and Cam.

"I think you're the man for the job." Easton held out his glass.

Hunt clinked it. He sure as hell hoped so.

"AND THEN, Hugo lured me right out of there." Harlow sipped her champagne. "There was a chase, a boat, a helicopter."

"That was me flying," a very pregnant Maggie Lopez-soon-to-be-Oliveira said from the couch. Savannah had learned the leggy brunette was the helicopter pilot for

Norcross Security, when she wasn't busy running her helicopter and drone business. The woman rubbed a hand over her large belly.

"The Norcross men and Easton all charged after me and saved the day." Harlow smiled. "And Easton told me that he loved me."

The look on the woman's face made Savannah itch for her sketchbook.

"I think my drama and the climax at the gala were even more dramatic," Princess Sofie said in her soft, European accent.

The woman was petite and elegant, with creamy skin, and strawberry-blonde hair in a classic French twist.

"Girl, I had a gun fight with the gun for hire." Gia flung an arm out. Miraculously, she didn't spill any of her champagne.

"Yes, yes, you were stuck in the middle of dangerous situations," Brynn said from her end of the couch, looking gorgeous in a little, black dress.

Savannah shook her head. "I won't lie, hearing all your stories, it makes me feel a little better about what's been happening to me."

Haven patted her shoulder.

Gia eyed Brynn. "You were in a dangerous situation, too."

Brynn sipped her beer. "Yes, but I was undercover. I'm a detective, and I had it under control."

Gia snorted. "Oh, so when my brother rescued you from a dangerous biker gang, and you guys went on the run, it was all under control?"

Brynn sniffed. "Yes."

The women all laughed.

"And when he swam across San Francisco Bay to infiltrate a ship to rescue you—"

"Hey, I'd already rescued myself." Brynn got a faraway look. "But that man is sure hot in a wet suit, or a business suit, or in jeans, and when he's naked."

Gia held up a hand. "No. No talking about my brother naked." She pointed at Haven and Harlow as well. "Any of them."

Savannah laughed. This was nice. She really liked Hunt's friends. It made her miss Saskia even more. Her bestie was a brilliant ballet dancer with a snappy wit.

"Now—" Gia's direct, brown gaze arrowed in on Savannah, and she fought the urge to duck behind Sofie. "I wouldn't mind hearing about Hunt naked. He's not a blood relative."

More feminine laughter.

"Well..." Savannah hedged.

"I've seen him naked," Brynn said. "And Ryder and Camden. It was a family holiday. I think Hunt was about twelve, and the boys snuck off to go skinny dipping in the river with my brother, Bard. It was a *very* enlightening experience for a young girl."

"Well, he's not twelve now." Savannah's gaze moved across the room to where the men gathered on the terrace. "Holy hell, they are a handsome lot."

"Tell me about it," Maggie murmured. "In their suits, or in ballistic vests, about to rappel out of my helo. They are all-too-delectable."

The women all looked at the men and nodded.

"And that Killian is something." Harlow fanned her

face. "There's just something about a dangerous man in a suit."

"Here's to our hot guys." Gia held up her champagne flute. "Not just the abs and tight asses—" more laughter "—but their tough, overprotective goodness."

They all clinked their glasses.

"Hunt looks at Savannah like he's starving," Haven said. "It's making me feel warm."

Savannah flushed. "Um, it's new."

"I've *never* seen him look at any woman that way," Brynn added.

Savannah glanced over at him. He was talking with Saxon and Vander. "I'm terrified he'll get hurt."

"Savannah—" Haven gripped her arm.

"My stalker *shot* at him. Walkson won't stop. He wants to destroy my life, and he'll go after anything I love or care about."

She saw understanding in Brynn's eyes. "So, you can't let yourself love."

Savannah shook her head. "Hunt is such a good man. A good brother, a good friend, an excellent cop. I...I won't be the reason he gets hurt, or worse."

The women shifted closer.

"Hunt is a very good cop," Gia said.

"There is no way that asshole Walkson can get the better of him," Brynn said.

"But Hunt plays fair and has to follow the rules," Savannah said. "Walkson doesn't."

Brynn grabbed Savannah's hand. "Listen to me. Hunt was Delta Force. That's badass. He's had training that Walkson can't even comprehend. And Hunt hasn't gone soft. He's a dedicated detective, and he keeps fit and is at the firing range weekly. He really can take care of himself."

Savannah nodded and licked her lips. "When he got shot—" God, her stomach turned in on itself "—it was the worst moment of my life."

"Even worse than when you were attacked by your stalker?" Harlow asked quietly.

"Yes."

From the couch, Maggie made a sound. "Savannah, I hate to tell you this, but you're already in love with Hunt."

Panic hit. It tasted hot and sticky and sharp in her throat. "*No*." She shook her head.

"Let her live in denial for a little longer." Gia patted Savannah's forearm.

"One other thing," Brynn said. "Hunt's not alone, Savannah." The woman nodded her head at the men. "He has his brothers and friends with him. They have his back. And each of them is a bona fide badass."

"But of course, Vander is the king of the badasses." Haven gave a little shiver. "He still kind of scares me a little."

Brynn eyed her man and smiled. "Yep."

Savannah let out a breath. "God, they are all so hot."

"I know," Harlow sighed. "I have to scare a couple of gold diggers off Easton a few times a week." She smiled. "It's a cross to bear for being the fiancée of a handsome billionaire."

"Yeah, you've got it rough." Maggie grinned as she sipped her alcohol-free cocktail.

Suddenly, Brynn's phone chimed. She pulled it out and frowned.

Across the room, Savannah saw Hunt do the same thing. Her gut knotted. "What is it?"

"A murder," Brynn said.

Hunt strode over and Savannah's belly did a sickening turn. "It's Walkson."

Hunt took her hand and pulled her out of the living area. They crossed the central landing and entered a more formal living room.

It was a cooler, more elegant space, with large windows that framed the Bay.

"Tell me," she whispered.

He cupped her cheeks. "There was a break-in at the De Winter. It's a small art museum."

"God."

"There's been a murder. A young, blonde woman, no ID yet."

Savannah jerked and Hunt pulled her close.

"Another death," she whispered.

"Which is on whoever killed her. We don't know that it's Walkson, yet."

But they both knew it was. She grabbed the lapels of Hunt's shirt. "This could be bait, to lure you out so he can get to you."

"I know. I'll take precautions, but I have to go."

She nodded reluctantly.

"Stay here," he said. "I'll come and get you after."

After he'd seen to a dead woman who needed justice.

Hunt kissed her. Vander and Brynn appeared in the door.

"Cam and I are coming, too," Vander said. "And Ace will put up a surveillance drone. This asshole won't take you by surprise again."

Brynn was right, they all had Hunt's back.

But that didn't stop Savannah's fear. She knew in her heart what Walkson was capable of.

"Stay safe." She gave Hunt another kiss, and then he and the others were gone. She turned and stared at the city lights. They blurred.

She felt so alone.

Then, the voices of the women sounded in the doorway. A moment later, they piled into the room.

Haven grabbed one of Savannah's hands and Harlow the other. Gia lifted her chin. "We're going to have another drink." Her firm tone dared anyone to argue.

Warmth cut through the ice in Savannah's chest.

Surrounded by support, she let them pull her out of the room.

CHAPTER FIFTEEN

Hunt walked into the De Winter Museum and took it in. It was a small place on the edge of Golden Gate Park that specialized in modern art.

Light from the police cruisers outside strobed through the plate-glass windows in red and blue.

"What the hell?" Cam muttered.

Hunt saw his brother eyeing a sculpture that looked like two people melted together and topped by colored circles that looked like fried eggs.

He liked Savannah's art style better.

He headed through an arch into the next room. Brynn and Vander followed right behind him.

Cam brought up the rear, alert as always. On the watch for any sign of Walkson.

Some officers were gathered in a small group. A young one looked pretty pale in the face, but was holding it together. You never forgot your first murder scene.

"Where's the victim?" Hunt asked.

"Through there," a female officer said. "It's a real mess, Detective."

"Who found her?"

"The cleaning crew. The museum was closed for the night and locked up tight. They come in to clean every night."

"ID?"

The officer nodded. "Eloise Walters. She works here part-time, and is a budding artist. She takes classes at the San Francisco Art Institute."

He noted her badge. "Thanks, Dempsey." Hunt dragged in a breath and strode through into the room.

In the center stood a pedestal holding a large, blue box, topped with a yellow sphere, topped with a small, green pyramid. The label said it was called *Finding Home.*

Beside him, Vander grunted.

"Not your style, Norcross?" Brynn asked.

"No."

Hunt took another step, and then he saw her. A spray of blood covered the wall. It almost looked like paint.

The woman lay sprawled on the glossy tile floor, her legs and arms askew like a broken doll.

Her skirt, once white, was now red. Her shirt was cut open and when he saw the fine slash marks—akin to the scars on Savannah's belly—his chest hardened.

"Her throat was cut," Brynn said dispassionately.

It wasn't that she didn't care. Hunt knew his cousin cared too much sometimes. No, in their job, they had to learn to switch off and compartmentalize. One, to get the job done, and two, to cope with the things that they saw.

"The murderer left you a message." Vander shifted, deftly avoiding the blood. He crouched.

Frowning, Hunt followed. His gut cramped.

Walkson had written on the wall, using the victim's blood.

"Asshole," Brynn muttered.

Yeah, he was.

Susannah is mine.

You can't have her.

Soon, I'll have her under my blade. Her sweet, red blood will flow for me.

You can't stop me.

You can't stop destiny.

Hunt's fingers curled into a fist. He fought hard to control his rage.

"The guy's totally unhinged," Brynn said. "He thinks Savannah is his destiny." Brynn shook her head.

"Walkson is *not* getting near her," Hunt growled.

Both Vander's and Brynn's heads whipped around.

"Deep breath, Hunt." Worry crossed Brynn's face.

Vander rose. "You can't lose it. She needs you to keep your head clear, so you can track Walkson down and lock him up."

"I'll kill him." Hunt's hand flexed.

In his job, he tried to be black-and-white and follow the rules. He was a cop. But he knew there was gray in the world as well. Hell, Vander made a career out of operating in the gray.

"Hunt..." Brynn's voice was full of concern.

"Walkson has murdered and terrorized across the damn country, and unfortunately, gotten away with it for years. He's ended the lives of promising young women, and he's destroyed Savannah's life. Why should he live?"

"Hey." Brynn grabbed Hunt's arm. "I know you're angry, and I know that under the mad is fear for Savannah. You aren't alone on this, Hunt."

Camden walked into the room and crossed his arms over his chest. He glanced at the victim, then the message, his scarred face grim.

"We're all with you on this," Vander said. "All of us. To help catch Walkson and help keep Savannah safe."

Hunt let out a breath. He pressed a hand over Brynn's and squeezed. His rage simmered down—still there, still white-hot—but in control enough so he could function.

"I'm falling in love with her." Hell, he was pretty much there.

Brynn's lips quirked. "Only just working that out? You're a good detective, Hunt, you should've realized."

Vander smiled. "I knew you'd go down eventually. Figured you'd do it before me, and have a house in the 'burbs."

"With a picket fence," Cam added. "And a pregnant wife."

The image of Savannah pregnant hit Hunt and he straightened. He imagined her at her easel, one of his shirts falling over her round belly.

Fuck. He dragged in air. He wanted that. Really wanted it.

"She'll fight me." He scraped a hand over his head. "Being on the run, it's made her skittish. It's taken a lot to get her to trust me. She ran to protect her mother and brother who she loves. She hasn't spoken to them for years."

"She just needs time to adjust," Cam said, an undertone to his voice. "But knowing Walkson is in jail will go a long way to helping her."

"The way she looks at you..." Brynn smiled. "She cares deeply, whether she wants to admit it or not."

"I'm afraid that when this is over, she'll leave, and go back to New York." There, Hunt's real fear was exposed. "She deserves the life she wants, that has been denied to her."

"Loving a woman is tough," Vander said.

Brynn slapped her man's arm.

But Vander caught her hand. "But it's worth every second of the pain, fear, risk and upheaval."

Brynn smiled. "Not a bad comeback, Norcross."

Hunt watched Vander place a quick kiss on Brynn's fingers, then Hunt turned his gaze back to the young woman who would never fall in love, or realize her dreams, or live her life.

For now, he had to stand for her.

Later, he'd make a plan for how to convince Savannah that he was in love with her, and that she was in love with him.

After he caught a murderer.

SAVANNAH PACED Easton and Harlow's living area. She couldn't sit still, or focus. Her belly was doing an uncomfortable dance.

It'd been doing that the entire time Hunt had been gone.

Damn Walkson to hell.

Most of the people had left. Murder tended to put a dampener on a party.

Ace had taken an exhausted Maggie home. Haven and Rhys had left, Haven hugging Savannah multiple times and trying to distract her with talk of a showing at the Hutton. Sofie and Rome had left, and then Gia and Saxon.

Now, Harlow was doing her best to keep Savannah from losing her mind.

Easton and Ryder were talking quietly in the kitchen.

"You have a beautiful home," Savannah said.

Harlow waved a hand. "It's all Easton. Like I mentioned earlier, my father got involved in some financial trouble, and I got pulled into it." A faint smile. "It's all resolved, thankfully. Easton moved me in here for my protection, and I never left. I've been adding my own stamp here and there." She cocked her head. "Watch out, because I highly doubt Hunt's going to let you move out of his place when this is all over."

Savannah's heart did a funny jig. "Oh, it's not like that."

Harlow's brows went up. "Really?"

"I mean, we're enjoying ourselves, but I drive him crazy. The man is very neat and proper. And a bit bossy."

"Mmm." Harlow didn't sound convinced.

"This—" Attraction? Desire? Inferno? "—will run its course." Savannah forced a laugh. "After dealing with my stalker, he'll probably be glad to see the back of me." And then he'd find some pretty, easy, sweet woman. Savannah frowned at the thought.

Harlow didn't laugh. "You don't really believe that."

Savannah dropped onto the couch, then jumped back up again. She couldn't sit. The butterflies in her stomach trying to head up into her throat. "Stop freaking me out more, Harlow."

"Okay. You need to fight it. I get it. I did, too."

Savannah let out a breath. "He got hurt because of me."

"Savannah—"

She shook her head, all the terrible emotions inside her swelling, coalescing into a horrible, spiky ball that felt like it was ripping at her insides. "People get hurt because of me. Today, a woman out there somewhere died a horrible, bloody death. All alone, her beautiful life gone. Just because she was an artist and has blonde hair like me."

"Oh, Savannah." There were tears in Harlow's eyes.

Savannah sensed the men moving closer.

"I can't love someone. I can't let them love me, or Walkson will make them pay for it—" Her voice cracked. She felt like the world was pushing down on her.

Suddenly, her legs gave way, but Ryder caught her.

"It's all right, babe. We're here. I've got you."

He felt and sounded so similar to Hunt.

"I can't let him get hurt." She clung to Ryder. "I have to protect him."

"He can take care of himself, and believe me, my brother is not going to walk away. He'll keep you safe, no matter what."

It was the *no matter what* part that she was afraid of.

"Another woman is dead." Grief hit, and sobs tore out of her.

Ryder's arms tightened. "Babe—"

Then suddenly he lifted her and spun.

And she found herself in Hunt's familiar arms.

"Hunt—"

"It's okay, Savannah." He sat on Easton and Harlow's couch, and pulled her onto his lap.

This seemed to be their favorite position. He was always offering her comfort. It seemed like she was always falling apart lately

"I'm not usually this weak."

He made an annoyed sound. "This is a sign of your strength. You've had to hold it together for so long, now, with me, you know you can fall apart. It's safe. I'll catch the pieces and help you put them back together."

Oh, God. She never knew men like Hunter Morgan existed. She pressed her face to his neck, and let her tears fall.

"Come on." He stroked her back. "Let's get back to the penthouse."

"I'll follow you guys back," Ryder said.

Savannah let Hunt bundle her into the Ferrari. They were both quiet on the drive back to the Four Seasons. She glanced at his shadowed face. His jaw was tight.

She'd been so lost in her own meltdown, that she hadn't thought how it was for him tonight. Seeing a murder. It must've been so horrible.

Finally, back in the safety of the penthouse, she kicked off her shoes and watched him pour a glass of bourbon.

He knocked one back, then poured another.

"It was bad?" she asked, quietly.

"It was bad." He sat on the couch.

"It was Walkson?"

Hunt nodded.

"What was her name?" Savannah asked.

"Eloise. She was an art student who worked part-time at the museum."

Savannah walked over and took a sip of his drink, then leaned down to kiss him.

"Thank you for taking care of her. For being her voice."

"Walkson will *not* touch you, Savannah. Not one hair on your head."

His tone made her shiver.

She saw in his eyes how bad the murder scene was. Suddenly, she was so angry. All her grief and sadness morphed.

"I'm *so* sick of Andrew Walkson. Fuck him." She spun and snatched an ornate paperweight off the coffee table. She threw it at the wall. She followed with a book, then a vase.

The vase smashed.

"Savannah." Hunt's arms wrapped around her.

"It always feels like he's one step ahead. In the driver's seat. I'm left to get tossed around, and I'm sick of it."

"It'll be over soon."

"It's *never* over." She broke free and grabbed his glass. She threw it at the wall. It broke into shards.

Hunt grabbed her.

"Let me have a tantrum, Hunter."

"I think you've ranted enough."

"No, I haven't." Then he wrestled her, and Savannah found herself flat on her back on the couch, with Hunt's big body on top of her.

"It's time to turn it off for a while," he said.

She let out a shuddering breath.

He pressed a kiss to her forehead. "You had a meltdown because you're worried about me."

"That's part of it." She gripped his biceps. "I should leave. He'd stop targeting you and the women of San Francisco if I did."

Hunt's body went rock-solid. "Fuck, no. You're not running." He pressed his angry face nose to nose with hers. "You're staying right here, with me, forever."

She went still. "What?"

"I'm in love with you," he growled.

A hundred different emotions stormed through Savannah. "No, you're not." Okay, her voice sounded totally panicked.

Green eyes flashed. "I am, and if you dig deep, you'd admit that you're in love with me, too."

Savannah sucked in a breath. "I am not. You can't tell me what I feel."

"I just did."

Her heart leaped around like crazy. "You are so stubborn."

"Yes. After I deal with Walkson, then I want you to marry me."

Savannah's chest locked and she couldn't breathe. "You've lost your mind, Morgan."

He looked smug. "No. I love you, so you'll just have to get used to hearing it."

He kissed her. She fought him for a second, but it was Hunt, so she caved.

She pulled him closer and kissed him back.

CHAPTER SIXTEEN

Hunt finished tying his tie, then pulled on his shoulder holster.

"God, you're hot."

He looked up. Savannah leaned against the doorjamb, wearing a black, silky robe and cradling a coffee mug.

Her cheeks were still flushed from their lovemaking session in the shower. He grabbed his SIG off the bedside table, checked it again, and slid it into the holster.

"Cam will be here soon," Hunt said. "He'll stay with you today."

She did a poor job of hiding the worry in her eyes.

Hunt took the mug and set it down. He cupped her cheeks. "I need you to trust me."

"I trust you. It's Walkson I don't trust."

"I'm meeting with Brynn and Killian. Killian's hacker got some info. We'll put pressure on him until Walkson has nowhere left to hide. We've sent his picture out to the stations. The local news is running a report that he's a person of interest in Eloise Walters' murder. Women will be wary. He'll have a harder time moving around and finding another victim."

Savannah bit her lip. "Okay, that's good. And you won't be alone today? You won't fall for any of Walkson's sneaky, underhanded tricks?"

Hunt kissed her. "No." *Mmm.* She tasted like coffee.

He kissed her again and backed her up. Her back hit the wall, and her robe fell open. His cock swelled and he cupped her breast, before boosting her up. He was happy to see her bruises were looking a little better.

She wrapped her legs around his waist. "God, every time I kiss you feels like the first." Her tongue dueled with his. "But better."

Hunt let his mouth travel down her neck, peppering kisses over her bruised skin, and felt her body rub against his. "I never stop wanting you."

His phone vibrated and he muttered a curse. Keeping her pinned, he pulled it out.

"Cam is on his way up. My brother always had bad timing."

Savannah smiled, and rubbed her body against his aching cock again. "You'll have to save it until later."

"Tease." He cupped her cheek. "I love you."

He saw the flash of fear in her eyes.

"I know you think you do," she whispered.

Pushing down his annoyance, edged with hurt, he set her down. He knew he had to fight to convince her.

He nipped her lips. "And you think I'm stubborn." He pulled her robe back into place. "Now get dressed. I don't want my brother seeing all of this beauty."

She rolled her eyes at him, but headed into the bathroom.

Hunt met Cam in the living area. "Hi."

Cam lifted his chin. "How's she doing?"

Hunt rubbed the back of his neck. "She's holding it together, but it's wearing on her. Of course, she's scared for everyone else but herself."

"You found a good one, Hunt. Beautiful, talented, and a decent person. Add in her strength, and it's a potent combination."

"Find your own woman."

Cam smiled, but it was a little sad. "I'm too broken."

Hunt stilled. "Cam—"

His brother held up a hand. "I find it hard to sleep through the night. I...I don't want to inflict my shit on a woman. If I need sex, a one-night stand will do the job. I'm good."

Hunt blew out a breath. "You're not good."

"Let's just focus on the stalker who's after you and your woman right now. Go. I've got her."

"Thanks, Cam." Hunt shifted closer. "And you have plenty to offer a woman. Don't let the shit in your head tell you differently. I've been there. Vander and the others have, too. It gets better, the battle readiness fades, and sleep gets a bit easier."

Cam kept Hunt's gaze, but didn't respond.

"Hi, Camden." Savannah appeared, eyeing them carefully.

She had dressed in black leggings, and a billowing top in a pretty shade of green.

"I'm headed out." Hunt crossed over and gave her a quick kiss. "Be good."

"Be safe."

Hunt drove to the Public Safety Building, a Norcross X6 driven by Saxon in tow.

It didn't matter that it was Sunday, the station was as busy as always. When he got to his office, Brynn and Killian were waiting for him.

"How's Savannah?" Brynn asked.

"She's okay." Hunt sat in his desk chair. "But I want this done. I want Walkson in jail, and paying for his crimes."

"The local stations are showing his picture, and we have all our officers on the lookout for him," Brynn said.

"My employee, Hex, has been doing some digging." Killian opened a sleek, high-tech laptop. "With Ace's help, she's accessed CCTV around San Francisco."

"You mean hacked," Hunt said.

Killian raised a dark brow. "Do you have a problem with that?"

"Fuck, no. As long as I can still put the fucker away, I don't care how we catch him."

Hunt would do anything to keep Savannah safe. It was a hell of a realization to know there was no line he wouldn't cross for her.

"They've caught glimpses of him," Killian said. "Not clear shots, the guy's wearing glasses to distort his face, and he does what he can to distort his height and build, but Hex's program is good at adjusting for that. We caught him near the De Winter Museum."

Hunt's pulse spiked. On screen was a map of the city,

littered with red dots. An image flashed up in a new window.

It showed a man, more shadow than anything else. He was on a darkened street near the De Winter. His shoulders were hunched, he was wearing a hoodie, and his face was obscured by a bright blur of light.

"These glasses are actually making it easier to spot him," Hunt said.

"Yes, there aren't many people walking around with anti-facial-recognition glasses on." Killian leaned forward. "There's a pattern to the sightings. They're clustered around Nob Hill."

"He's staying there, somewhere," Hunt said.

Killian smiled. "I believe so."

Another window popped open on the screen, and a woman appeared. "Hey, boss man."

"Hex," Killian said.

The woman was fine-boned, with short, black hair tipped with pale pink. She grinned and waved. Brynn waved back, and Hunt nodded.

"Detective Hunter Morgan, Detective Brynn Sullivan, this is Jet "Hex" Adler."

Hex winked at Hunt. "They make detectives mighty fine on the West Coast."

"He's taken," Killian said.

"The good ones always are. I've got something on your perp." Hex pulled a face. "Now, I'm just saying, this guy you're after is a dirtbag loser. I look forward to you nailing his ass to the wall."

"Hex," Killian prompted.

"Right. We just got a ping on Walkson from that

sexy, hunkalicious Norcross hacker, and yes, I know he's taken, too."

Hunt straightened in his chair. "Where?"

"In the Nob Hill area. Mason Street. There are several hotels in the vicinity. Boss, I've emailed you the list."

Hunt rose. "I'll round up a couple of uniforms and start searching."

Brynn smiled. "This could be it. We could arrest him today."

Hunt sure as hell hoped so. "Let's move."

THE SUNSHINE WAS LOVELY.

Savannah was out on the penthouse terrace, enjoying the light breeze. She had her easel set up. With a palette knife, she was daubing colors on the canvas, bringing her picture to life.

Camden was sprawled on the outdoor couch nearby. He didn't say much, but the silences weren't awkward.

They'd eaten a simple lunch together, and realized they had a shared love of mustard on everything. She eyed him out of the corner of her eye. There was an edginess to him. Like he was waiting for a bear to burst out of the nicely manicured plants and attack.

"I can feel you watching me," he said.

"I'm an artist, I watch everyone."

He made a purely masculine sound. "This face isn't pretty enough for you to paint."

Savannah lowered her knife. "Cam, you have to know

that you are plenty easy on the eyes. You and your brothers have that good-looking, all-American-man-thing going on. I bet you were a quarterback in high school and all the cheerleaders chased you."

"I was a running back."

"That still makes my point."

He shrugged one broad shoulder. "They wouldn't be chasing anymore." He waved at his scarred cheek.

It wasn't nearly as bad as he probably thought.

"To the right woman, that makes you more attractive. It shows you've lived, survived, all while serving your country." She dabbed her knife in the paint.

Cam cocked his head. "I see why my brother likes you. You sure have him tied up in knots."

"And I can see you're changing the subject." She bit her lip. "Any word from Hunt?"

Cam shook his head. "I wasn't expecting to hear anything, so just chill, Savannah."

She tried to relax her shoulders. "Sure."

He eyed her canvas. It was an embracing couple, the darker-skinned man was much taller than the slim woman he held, who wore a flowing dress the same color as her strawberry-blonde hair.

"Rome and Sofie," Cam said.

Savannah nodded. The Norcross gang gave her plenty of inspiration. She was planning to do Easton and Harlow next.

A cell phone rang from inside.

"That's mine." She set her knife down.

She followed the sound to the coffee table. It was a

number she didn't recognize. Frowning, she answered. "Hello?"

"Hello, Susannah."

That pleasant, normal voice shouldn't strike terror in her. Her hand clenched on the phone.

She turned away from the terrace doors. "Fuck you, asshole. You're going down, and it's just a matter of time. I look forward to sitting in court, listening as they sentence you to die in prison. It's not so comfy there, Andrew."

"Hmm, I see that big thug of a cop that you're fucking has made you overconfident."

Time to tell Cam about the call. She took one step toward the terrace doors—

"I have someone here with me. A friend of yours."

Savannah froze.

"If you tell anyone that I'm on the phone with you, I'll slit her throat. You can listen to her scream."

Savannah couldn't breathe. Cam appeared in the open door.

She forced a smile. "It's Harlow. Girl talk."

With a grunt, he disappeared back onto the terrace.

"You're just tormenting me," she whispered furiously. "Your photo is all over the news. Hunt's tracking you down."

Walkson made an unhappy sound. "Yes, I figured I had your lover to thank for that. I will kill him, Susannah. You should never have let him touch what is *mine*."

"I'm not yours!" she whisper-yelled. "I never was, and I never will be."

"I saw it in your art. We're meant to be. Destined."

"You need help, and you need to be punished for the women you murdered."

"They didn't mean anything. And this sweet thing with me, she's just a stand-in for you. I'll send you a picture."

"I don't want anything from you—"

The phone dinged in her hand. An incoming message. Mouth dry, she thumbed the screen and then her throat closed.

The image on the screen sent Savannah's world tumbling to her feet.

A terrified Ella-Mae was in the shot with a smiling Walkson beside her.

The teenager's mouth was gagged, her eyes pleading and afraid.

No. *No.* This couldn't be happening. Nausea slammed into Savannah. She swallowed, fighting the urge to vomit.

"Ella-Mae," Savannah whispered brokenly.

"She's a sweet, sweet young thing. Now, you come to me, and I'll let her go."

Savannah's stomach contracted to a hard, sharp point. Her skin flushed hot.

"If you don't come to me, Susannah, she dies. Her blood spills while she screams and cries your name."

Muffled whimpers came across the line.

Savannah squeezed her eyes closed. She remembered Ella-Mae's smile, all the girl's questions about art, her shyly telling Savannah about a boy she liked, running to get Hunt to help Savannah deal with John Garoppolo.

Ella-Mae was innocent.

"Come to me, Susannah. And this sweet thing can go home."

Savannah pulled in a harsh breath. "Where?"

An excited chuckle. "I've rented out a little studio. I'm not telling you exactly where it is, because that cop of yours will probably listen to this conversation. If you let them discover where I am, Ella-Mae dies. So, all I'll tell you, is *you'll* be able to work out where I'm at. Think hard. Think about your art, and us being together."

What the hell did that mean?

"We'll have the studio all to ourselves. But get here fast, or I'll start cutting Ella-Mae's milky-white skin."

"Don't you dare touch her. I'm coming."

"Oh, and Susannah? If you tell that thug in your bed, or any of the other guard dogs around you, she dies. She dies painfully."

"Okay."

"See you soon." He ended the call.

Savannah stared out the window, feeling desolate inside. If she told Hunt, he and Vander would try to rescue Ella-Mae.

And if Walkson caught wind, he would kill her. And he'd enjoy it. He'd enjoy Ella-Mae's pain, and Savannah's despair.

She couldn't tell Hunt, not until Ella-Mae was safe.

Walkson wouldn't kill Savannah straightaway. If Ella-Mae got free, then there would be time for Hunt and the others to rescue Savannah.

She dragged in a breath. *Right.* Now she needed to slip away from Camden.

"Savannah?" Her bodyguard appeared, frowning at her. "Everything all right with Harlow?"

"Sorry." Savannah shook her head. "Yes, everything's fine. I just got an idea for a sculpture that I want to do."

He nodded.

"I'm going to make some coffee." She jerked a thumb toward the kitchen. "And visit the powder room. You want a cup of coffee?"

"Sure."

"Go back and soak up the sunshine. I'll bring it right out."

He eyed her for a second, then went back onto the terrace.

The air rushed out of her. She set the coffee maker working, then slipped into the powder room.

She was well aware that she needed every advantage to sneak past Cam. She turned on the faucet and looked in the mirror.

She looked pale and afraid.

Ella-Mae's depending on you. Savannah had to work out where the hell this studio was. Something to do with her art and Walkson.

Get out first, then work on the puzzle. With the coffee maker and the water running, it should hide the noise of the elevator.

She darted out. There was no sign of Cam. Her heart thundered.

She pressed the button. "Come on. Come on."

There was a discreet ding, but to her it sounded like the clash of cymbals.

The doors opened, and she stepped inside. She

decided to get off a few floors from the bottom and take the stairs, just in case Cam worked out that she was in the elevator.

The doors closed and the elevator descended.

Hold on, Ella-Mae.

CHAPTER SEVENTEEN

Air sawed in and out of her lungs.

Savannah jogged down the stairs, circled the landing, and kept going.

Fear jumped in her gut. She didn't want to go *anywhere* near Walkson, but she was more afraid for Ella-Mae.

Savannah had to move faster, and work out where the hell the studio was.

Think, Savannah, think.

More so she was afraid that Camden, or one of the Norcross men would catch her. These guys were ridiculously good at their jobs.

She paused for a second to catch her breath.

Hunt would be so mad.

Her chin dropped. God, she had no choice, but she felt terrible. He'd done so much to keep her safe, but Ella-Mae's life was what mattered right now.

Savannah heard a door slam in the stairwell above and that spurred her into action. Finally, she reached the ground level and opened the door. She peeked out and watched people milling around the busy lobby. She slipped out, careful to walk slowly and steadily.

Then she spotted Saxon near the front doors on his cell phone, his face looking serious.

Oh, shit.

A maintenance man was pushing a cart toward the door, loaded with what looked like doorframes. She slipped around on the other side, so he blocked Saxon's view of her. It was flimsy, but it was all she could manage. She kept the man's body between her and Saxon.

The elevator dinged, and her breath caught.

"Camden's here," Saxon growled into the phone. "We'll find her, you just work on finding out who that call was from."

Savannah stepped outside.

She didn't have long. She powered down the street. She had to move fast, or the Norcross men would stop her.

She picked up speed, almost jogging. She neared an intersection, watching as a cable car moved past her.

Something made her look back.

Her rabbiting heart leaped into her throat.

Camden was sprinting down the sidewalk toward her. His face was focused, his strong arms pumping.

Oh. *God.*

Savannah turned and darted across the street. A car slammed on the brakes, tires screeching. Someone laid on the horn. She ran as fast as she could.

She did a quick look back.

Cam was gaining. Her heart hit her ribs. She

watched him reach the stopped car and slide across the hood—powerful, athletic.

She'd never outrun him. She pushed for more speed, lungs burning, and saw that she was almost at the cable car. It was at the crest of a hill, just about to begin its descent.

Cam was getting closer.

Savannah leaped onto the back of the moving cable car and grabbed a pole.

As she watched, the cable car pulled away. A car pulled out of a side street and slammed on the brakes, almost hitting Cam. He slowed and she saw him curse.

I'm sorry.

"Lady, are you all right?" a man asked.

"Um, my ex is after me. He's...not nice."

"Jesus." The guy nodded. "You're safe now. Take a seat and catch your breath."

She gave him a wan smile, sorry for lying to him.

She pulled out her phone. She needed to find the studio. Her belly cramped. *Come on. Come on.* Ella-Mae's life was depending on her.

What about her art—?

It hit her like a bolt of lightning. The first piece Walkson bought from her. She quickly did a search for art studios in the area and found a list. She spotted the name and address and knew instantly that it was the right place.

Her belly cramped. It wasn't far away. She needed to get off in a few more stops.

Her phone rang and she jolted, and almost dropped it.

Hunt's name was on the screen.

God. She pressed the phone to her temple. She wanted to hear his voice, but he'd talk her out of this.

She couldn't let Ella-Mae pay the price. Savannah pressed the screen and it stopped the ringing. She tapped in a message.

I'm sorry.

What the fuck, Savannah?

He has Ella-Mae. I have to help her.

God, there was so much she wanted to say to him.

Stay where you are.

I'll get her to contact you when she's free. Let me get her out of there first.

Savannah turned her phone off. She had no doubt that Ace could track her.

Her head bowed. She hated that Hunt would be so worried and mad. Her stomach swirled and she felt sick.

She glanced out and saw her stop. The cable car slowed.

Savannah left her phone on the seat and leaped off. She hurried down the street. People passed by, going about their business, no clue that she was on her way to confront a killer.

Ahead, she saw the sign for the Infinity Studio.

She bit her lip hard, tasted blood.

The art studio looked nice. It had plate-glass

windows, and sage-green trim. A pretty, watercolor landscape hung in the window.

It didn't look like it was hiding something ugly.

She dragged in a breath, and she casually walked past, but didn't see anyone inside.

But he was in there. He could be hurting Ella-Mae right now.

Then she squared her shoulders and pushed open the studio door.

HUNT HAD NEVER FELT this afraid before. He sped toward the Norcross office, his brain turning every bloody crime scene he'd ever seen over in his head.

All the possibilities of what could happen to Savannah.

He knew just what damage a man could inflict on a woman.

Savannah was walking into the hands of a killer. One who was obsessed with her.

Hunt's woman was in danger.

He screeched into the lower-level parking at the Norcross office and leaped out of the car. He took the stairs two at a time.

The office was in upheaval. The men were crowded around the door to Ace's office.

Cam came straight toward Hunt, his face a terrible mask. "Hunt, I'm sorry. It's my fucking fault she got away."

Hunt gripped his brother's arm. "This is Walkson's

fault. You were there to protect her, you had no idea he'd get to her and she'd sneak out." Hunt drew in a breath. He planned to have a long, angry conversation with Savannah about her actions.

But a part of him got where her head was at. Walkson was a manipulative bastard, and he'd taken someone Savannah cared about, an innocent. Savannah was used to depending on herself and going it alone.

Well, not anymore. He'd make her accept that.

After he got her back safely.

"For now, we focus on getting her back. You with me?"

Cam nodded.

Now Hunt just had to follow that advice.

"Hunt." Vander eyed him carefully. "How are you holding up?"

"I'll be better once we have her back."

Brynn jogged up the stairs. "I got your message." She moved over and hugged Hunt. "We'll find her."

He gave his cousin a tight nod.

Brynn gave Vander a quick kiss. "I confirmed that Ella-Mae Birbeck never made it to her summer job today. It looks like she was snatched off the street, somewhere."

"He would've lured her," Hunt said. "Posed as an art dealer or gallery owner interested in her work. The asshole has an unassuming face."

Brynn nodded. "Women trust him."

"Savannah got a call. I knew something was off." Cam pressed a hand to his hip. "I should've trusted my instincts, but I've been trying to calm myself down. To not read danger in every little thing. She blew me off, said it was Harlow."

Ace strode out of his office, tablet in hand. "It wasn't Harlow. It was a call from a burner phone." He thumbed the screen and the call played.

"Hello, Susannah."

Hunt clenched his teeth. He listened to the conversation and Walkson's smarmy tone, Savannah's fear.

The call ended.

"An art studio she would know?" Hunt frowned.

"I've already set up searches to see if anything pops with studios here in San Francisco," Ace said.

"Maybe there's one with the same name as the gallery where she had showings in New York?" Brynn suggested.

Ace shook his head. "I already checked. Nothing came up. I've also looked up all versions of her name and Walkson's name."

"Hunt, can you think of anything?" Vander asked.

Hunt ground his teeth together. "No."

"Okay, let's hope the search hits something," Ace said.

"For now, we'll start researching studios around Nob Hill," Vander said. "We work in pairs. Ace will send everyone the list. Hunt, you're with me."

Brynn and Saxon headed out. Cam was paired with Rhys. Hunt strode across the open plan space. It was like he had a rock in his chest, pressing harder and harder against his lungs, his heart. He tried to lock down his fear-drenched rage.

It was how he'd felt when he'd heard what had happened to Manny, Eric and Mitchell.

"Hunt?" Vander's deep voice.

"Searching one by one will take too long. That murderous asshole has her."

"We'll get her back. Don't lose hope." Vander grabbed his shoulder. "I know exactly how hard that is."

Yes, Vander had been through it before, when Brynn had been taken by a dangerous biker gang. But Brynn was a trained cop.

"Savannah's smart," Vander said. "And she knows how to survive. She's focused on freeing the girl, then she'll be waiting for you to rescue her."

Hunt released a shuddering breath.

Vander squeezed his shoulder. "Keep it together, and let's go find your woman."

Hunt nodded. Soon he was in the passenger seat of an X6, as Vander drove them to Nob Hill.

Hold the fuck on, Savannah. Hunt stared through the windshield and hoped to hell they found the studio soon.

He couldn't lose her.

THE FRONT of the studio was empty. Savannah's heart pounded in her ears, her footsteps echoing quietly. There were nice pieces of art on the walls, but she was too scared and distracted to take them in. The silence in the space made her fear ratchet up.

It was probably what Walkson wanted. She should've had some sort of plan, but her brain wouldn't think clearly.

She swallowed, and headed toward the back.

There was a narrow hall, with some gear stacked on one side: paints, brushes, canvases, palette knives.

Her pulse spiked. She grabbed one of the knives and slid it into the pocket of her shirt.

Now, she was sorry she hadn't admitted how she felt about Hunter.

God. She pressed a hand to the wall. She loved her detective. Her big, solid, protective detective.

She shouldn't have let fear hold her back. She should've told him.

Dammit, she wanted the chance to tell him.

"Susannah?" Walkson's voice echoed down the hall. "I knew you'd come to me."

The bastard sounded so smug. She'd come because he'd threatened an innocent, teenaged girl, not because she wanted to be with him.

Savannah walked down the hall and stepped into the back room.

Ella-Mae was tied to a chair and gagged. When the girl saw Savannah, her eyes went wide, swimming with emotion.

"It's going to be all right, Ella-Mae." Savannah tried to keep her voice steady.

The room had been set up for artists to work in. There was an empty easel, potting wheel, shelves stocked with equipment, and drying racks. Walkson stood close to Ella-Mae, smiling.

"It's so good to see you, Susannah."

Savannah's insides turned to ice. He looked almost the same as the first time she'd met him at her very first showing. Brown hair, normal, plain face, slender build.

He could be anyone's son, cousin, friend. An accountant, computer programmer, a store manager.

If only he looked evil, then people could've seen the rot inside him sooner.

"How did you find me in San Francisco?" she asked.

He grinned. "It was luck. *Destiny.* A man I sold insurance to in New York, he showed me photos his mother had posted on social media. Of the lovely painting of flowers her sweet, friendly neighbor had painted for her."

Savannah sucked in a breath. Mrs. Romero. *God.*

"And the shooting at the coffee shop?" she asked. "The man who broke into my place?"

Walkson winked. "I just wanted to scare you a little. Punishment for running from me."

She shook her head. He was a monster.

Then she saw the knife in his hand, with blood dripping off it.

Savannah tensed. *No.* She looked back at Ella-Mae and saw blood on the girl's shirt.

"You hurt her?"

"Just one little cut." He smiled. "Nothing like what I gave you."

"I'm here now, so let her go."

He walked behind Ella-Mae's chair and stroked the girl's hair. She whimpered behind her gag.

"I'm not sure. She's such a pretty thing. And so frightened."

Savannah gritted her teeth. "You said if I came, you'd let her go."

Walkson frowned, his face turning angry. "Yes, but

I'm very mad at you Susannah. I think I need to punish you."

She tried to stay calm. "You said you'd let her go. I'm here. It's me you want."

"Yes, but I'm *angry*." He stroked Ella-Mae's cheek. The teenager tried to pull away. "You ran from me for so long. And then you let *him* touch you. That big, overgrown pig."

Savannah slid her hand into her pocket. Her hand curled around the hilt of the palette knife. Her pulse raced and she tried to focus. "I love him."

"No, you love me!" Walkson's face twisted. "You're meant for me. Your art, the paintings you did, it was all for *me*."

She bit her lip. Ella-Mae's terrified, pleading gaze was locked on hers. "You need help—"

"I'm not crazy!" He whirled and kicked at an easel, knocking it over. It slammed into the wall.

"I didn't say that." Savannah kept her voice low and even. "Let Ella-Mae go, and we'll talk."

"You care more about her than me. You care more about that cop than me. About everyone more than me!" He whipped the knife up and pressed it to Ella-Mae's cheek.

"No!" Savannah cried.

Tears rolled down the teenager's cheeks.

"Please let her go," Savannah said. "I'll do anything."

Walkson cocked his head. "You'll do anything for me?"

"Yes." Her stomach did a sickening turn.

He ran the tip of the knife down the girl's cheek and a thin, red line of blood appeared.

Then he cut her gag off.

"*Savannah*." Ella-Mae let out a wild sob.

"Don't call her that." Walkson yelled. He untied the girl's bindings. "Her name is Susannah."

"Just go, Ella-Mae." Savannah steeled herself. "I want to be with Andrew. You need to go."

She tried to urge the girl with her eyes to run as far and fast as she could.

Go and find Hunt.

Ella-Mae nodded, then stumbled past Savannah and into the hall.

Her running footsteps faded to nothing.

Savannah let out a breath. Ella-Mae was safe.

She looked at the smiling man who'd stalked and terrified her for years. Her hand tightened on the knife in her pocket.

She was done running. She was done being afraid.

"It's just you and me now, Andrew."

CHAPTER EIGHTEEN

Driving away from yet another art studio—this one packed with budding artists attending a class, Hunt bit back his frustration.

Walkson had already had Savannah too long.

Hunt would kill the man if he'd hurt her.

What if Hunt didn't make it in time? What if he wasn't there for her when it mattered, just like he wasn't there for Eric, Manny, and Mitchell?

"Hunt, stay with me," Vander said from the driver's seat.

"I've got a lock on it." A shaky lock. "It could take days to check all these studios. The one he's using might not even be listed."

"We're going to find her."

Vander's phone rang and he touched the screen on the dash.

"Vander." Ace's voice came through the speaker. "I've got something."

"What?" Hunt demanded.

"Before Savannah turned off her phone, she did some searches on art studios. Hex had a nifty program and could zero in where Savannah stopped scrolling. Do these words mean anything? Bryant, Midway, Electra, Infinity—"

Hunt sucked in a breath. "Wait. Infinity. It's a name of a painting she did. Fuck. It was the first piece that Walkson purchased of hers."

"There's an Infinity Studio in Nob Hill."

"Address," Vander barked. "Tell the others."

Ace rattled it off.

Vander took the next corner fast, tires screeching. He sped down the street, and the traffic thickened. Hunt bit back a curse

"It's not far," Vander said.

"You need to stop a block away. We don't want Walkson to know we're there."

Vander nodded.

Soon, they screeched into a parking spot on the street. Both men flung the doors open and Hunt started down the sidewalk.

"Hunt," Vander said.

Hunt looked up and saw a terrified Ella-Mae sprinting down the sidewalk. Her blonde-brown hair flew out behind her.

"Ella-Mae!" he yelled.

The sobbing teenager saw him, adjusted course, and then threw herself at him.

"It's okay. I've got you. Take some deep breaths."

Shit, there was blood on her cheek and shirt. She had no shoes on. "How badly are you hurt?"

"Not bad..." Her voice was unsteady. She gripped Hunt's jacket. "He has Savannah. She came in and made him let me go."

"I need to go and get her," Hunt said.

Ella-Mae nodded, tears streaming down her face. "Savannah needs you. That guy is crazy."

"Where are they in the studio?"

"The back room."

"Ella-Mae, I'm Hunt's friend, Vander." Vander held out a key fob. "There's a black BMW X6 parked down the street. Go and wait in it. I'll have people come to get you."

The teenager nodded, her fingers closing around the fob. "Go. Go and save Savannah."

Hunt and Vander broke into a jog.

"Plan?" Vander asked.

"Did Ace send you schematics of the studio?"

"Yeah." Vander pulled out his phone. "There's a main area in front, and a hall to the back room."

"Let's go in quietly." Hunt spotted the studio and pulled out his SIG.

Vander did the same.

Hunt slowly opened the front door. Vander slid inside, moving like a ghost. Hunt followed, easing the door closed behind him.

They moved through the front room, past the artwork on display.

They reached the hall and paused. A muffled

murmur of voices in the back caught his ear. One was definitely female, and one had the lower pitch of a man.

Vander gave a hand signal. They slowly moved down the hall. The conversation became clearer.

"I just wanted us to be together, Susannah. The way it's supposed to be."

"No, Andrew, you've concocted a fantasy. You don't even know me."

The sound of her voice made Hunt weak.

She was alive.

"I love you!" Walkson yelled.

A muscle ticked in Hunt's jaw.

"And I'm in love with someone else," she said. "Someone good and honorable, someone who helps people. He doesn't hurt them."

Hunt's chest locked. She loved him.

"Shut up about him!"

There was the sound of a scuffle. Hunt surged forward and bumped some canvases stacked against the wall. Several fell with a crash.

"Someone's here!" Walkson yelled.

Fuck. Hunt and Vander leaped forward.

The door to the back room slammed closed in their faces.

Hunt grabbed the door handle and rattled it. *Locked.*

"Savannah!" He rammed his shoulder against it.

"Hunt! He's locked the door—"

She broke off and there was the sound of fighting.

Fuck. He met Vander's gaze. "We need to get this door open. Now!"

"HUNT!"

Savannah dodged Walkson. He'd locked the door, dammit.

"He can't have you," Walkson barked.

"I'll give myself to whoever I want. You can't just take someone; you can't steal their life."

Walkson grabbed a heavy, marble pedestal for displaying art, then with a grunt, tipped it over. It landed in front of the door.

There were two loud gun shots and Savannah gasped. She saw the lock was gone. The door rattled, but the pedestal blocked it from opening.

Walkson smiled. "It's just you and me, Susannah."

She snatched up some jars filled with brushes and threw them at him.

He screamed and lunged at her. She leaped to the side, and grabbed a small box and swung it at his head.

It crashed into his nose and blood sprayed.

Adrenaline surged through her veins. *How do you like that, asshole?*

With an enraged roar, Walkson charged again. He tackled her, and they tumbled to the wood floor.

Ow. Her head hit the ground hard, leaving her dazed.

She heaved and they wrestled against each other, each of them trying to get on top. She shoved Walkson off, and scrambled to her feet, her chest heaving.

The door vibrated under a heavy hit.

Hunt was trying to get in.

She needed to try and move that damn pedestal, but Walkson was between her and the door.

Her stalker stared at her, blood running down his face. "He can't have you. I'll kill him."

Savannah laughed. She was *so* done being afraid of this man. "Hunter is ex-special forces, and a cop. He'll wipe the floor with a coward like you."

Walkson's lips flattened. "I'll cut him open in front of you, and make him scream."

"He's not alone, Walkson—"

"Andrew! You call me Andrew."

"No," she snapped. "It's over. Hunt isn't some defenseless, young woman. I'm not a defenseless, young woman. Not anymore." She pulled the palette knife out of her pocket and brandished it. "Today, you go to jail. And I walk out of here with Hunter. Tonight, I'll be crying out his name as he makes love to me."

Walkson made a horrible, animalistic sound. "You're *mine*."

He rushed her again. She slashed out with the knife, but he rammed his hand into her arm. The knife flew out of her fingers and hit the floor.

No!

He grabbed her shirt and they spun. They rammed into another empty pedestal and the corner dug into her back. He shoved her again and the pedestal toppled with a crash.

"Savannah!" Hunt roared through the door.

"He won't love you like I do," Walkson said.

"God, I hope not." She needed to get that door unblocked.

She grabbed a paint pot and the loose lid fell off. As Walkson advanced, she tossed it at him.

Blue paint splattered over his face and chest. She tried to dodge past him, but he sidestepped and blocked her.

Damn.

Walkson swiped the paint out of his eyes. "I'm losing patience with you, Susannah."

"It's *Savannah.* I left that younger, innocent artist behind. I'm tougher now, a survivor." She smiled as the door vibrated under another hit. "And that man out there loves me. True love, not your obsessive version. Not the sick thing you're offering. I have *so* much to live for."

A bunch of emotions crossed Walkson's face. "If I can't have you, no one will."

She froze. His voice was devoid of emotion.

The killer had made an appearance.

Oh, hell. She needed to get that door open.

Walkson lifted his knife, stained with Ella-Mae's blood.

Savannah drew in a breath. *Stay calm.*

Her stalker ran at her.

She grabbed the chair Ella-Mae had been tied on and threw it at him. She raced for the door.

"No!" Walkson kicked her legs out from under her.

She hit the floor with an oof, belly first.

The door was only a few feet away. She spun and saw Walkson coming at her. She kicked at him, and he slashed down with the knife. She rolled.

He slashed again and she rolled the other way.

Her heart drummed in her chest and that's when she

saw the palette knife she'd dropped before. She snatched it and swung it up.

It stabbed into the side of his neck.

He staggered back, a look of blank shock on his face.

Savannah scrambled up. She had to move that pedestal. "Let me move the—"

A hand grabbed the back of her shirt and yanked her backward.

Dammit. She fell and rolled, and saw Walkson looming above her.

He sliced down with his knife and stabbed her in the stomach.

THE WOODEN DOOR finally gave way and Hunt broke through the splintered wood. He charged in, Vander right behind him.

A bloody, paint-splattered Walkson had Savannah pinned to the floor. Hunt watched in horror as the man stabbed his knife down and into Savannah's belly.

No. A red haze covered Hunt's vision.

He whipped his SIG up and fired. The bullet hit Walkson in the shoulder, and the man jerked.

Then Hunt closed the distance and slammed his fist into the man's face.

Walkson yelped. Hunt punched the man again, and again. He kept punching, driving Walkson to the floor.

"Hunt," Vander barked.

The haze cleared a little. The killer was sprawled on

the floor, bleeding from the bullet wound in his shoulder, his face a bloody mess from Hunt's fist, and sobbing.

Hunt wanted to keep going. Wanted to punish him—for the lives he'd taken, for touching and terrorizing Savannah.

"Hunter?" Savannah's pain-filled voice snapped him all the way back.

He saw Vander crouched beside her. Hunt's friend had a rag pressed to her stomach. A bloody knife rested on the floor.

Her gray gaze locked on Hunt's face.

"Savannah." As he shifted beside her, Vander rose and stalked over to Walkson.

He toed the man and Walkson groaned.

"I...need a doctor."

"Be thankful I don't gut you," Vander said silkily.

Walkson's mouth snapped shut.

Vander lifted his cell phone and looked at the screen. "Brynn's on the way. With the cavalry."

Hunt focused on Savannah. "Baby." He pressed the rag down.

"I knew you'd come," she whispered. "I knew you'd work it out, or Ella-Mae would find you."

"I'm pissed at you."

"You can't be, I'm injured. You need to nurse me back to health." She winced. "It really, really hurts."

"You shouldn't antagonize serial killer stalkers with knives."

She gave a hiccupping, slightly hysterical, laugh. "Ella-Mae?"

"She got out."

Savannah's breath was shaky. "Good. Facing him, I wasn't terrified anymore. I'm so sick of him dictating my life." She cupped Hunt's cheek. "And I realized I had something, someone, really important to live for."

"Say the words," he said huskily.

"I love you, Hunter Morgan."

"I love you too, Savannah Cole." He pressed a gentle kiss to her lips.

Then Brynn burst in, handgun in hand. Cam, Rhys, Saxon, and several police officers were right behind her.

"Clear," Brynn barked.

A moment later, several paramedics appeared.

"She has a stab wound," Hunt said.

The officers headed toward Walkson, while the paramedics nodded, and got to work on Savannah.

Hunt shifted.

"Don't leave me," she said.

"Never." He took her hand. "After this, when you're better, I'm going to yell at you, and paddle your ass for sneaking out to meet a killer."

"I had to save Ella-Mae."

"Then I'll tell you how damn brave you are, and beautiful, and how you're going to marry me."

There was no fear in her eyes this time, just a smile.

"Nice to see you aren't so panicked by that," he said.

"I just got stabbed by my stalker, nothing can shake me now."

Shit. Just remembering his terror, knowing she was locked in with Walkson, made it hard to breathe.

Knowing how much danger she'd been in... He squeezed her fingers.

"It doesn't look too bad," the paramedic said. "From what I can tell, it missed anything vital, and you don't have any internal bleeding. We'll give you some painkillers and get you to the hospital for a more thorough check."

Savannah frowned. "Hospital? Can't you just glue it, or something?"

"Nope," the paramedic said cheerfully. "Hospital for you."

"Hunter—"

"Baby, no matter how much you plead, I want the doctors to check you over."

Her fingers clenched on his. "I'll cook for a month, I'll promise you sexual favors..."

The paramedic chuckled.

Hunt kissed her temple. "As tempting as that is, I'll cook for you until you're better, and when you're healed, you'll give me sexual favors anyway."

"Dammit," she muttered.

Another paramedic rolled a gurney in.

"The other guy's going first," Savannah's paramedic said.

Hunt didn't bother to watch them shift a now-handcuffed and sobbing Walkson to the gurney.

Brynn stopped and crouched by Hunt, touching his shoulder. "I'll escort Walkson to prison. Savannah, I'll see you soon."

Savannah nodded. "Thanks, Brynn."

"And I'll stay with you," Hunt told Savannah. "Every minute."

She smiled weakly. "Promise?"

"Baby, if you haven't worked it out yet, I'd do anything for you."

"God, I'm so in love with you."

He kissed the end of her nose. "I love you, too."

CHAPTER NINETEEN

The next day, Savannah sank back on the couch and laughed.

Ryder smiled at her. On him, the smile was slow, sexy, and designed to drive a woman to make bad mistakes.

"Okay, lie back and let me check your wound, babe. You know you want to get your clothes off for me."

"Stop flirting," she countered.

He winked at her. Despite his teasing, he was brisk and professional as he lifted her shirt. Charming demeanor aside, he was clearly good at his job.

She noted that he paid no attention to her old scars, just zeroed in on her wound. Thankfully, the hospital had confirmed that the knife had missed anything vital.

Andrew Walkson was in jail. He was in the medical wing at the prison, getting his neck wound monitored, and awaiting trial.

He was locked up, as Hunt had promised, and would never be a free man again.

A weight had lifted, but to be honest, she couldn't quite believe it yet. She'd been living on the edge for so long, and it was hard to let go. To relax and trust that she was safe.

She rubbed her temple and blew out a breath. "It's hard to believe it's over."

"It gets easier," Camden said from a stool at the island. "Eventually, you start to lose the fight or flight mode. And trust that you don't have to watch your six all the time."

"Quit reading my mind," she said.

He shrugged a broad shoulder. "Or so they say. So far, it seems to get a little bit better every day."

Warmth hit her. She hadn't realized what she had in common with Hunt's youngest brother.

"Thanks, Cam. I'm so sorry I snuck out on you."

His lips quirked. "A girl is alive because you did, but it still stings to know you pulled it off."

She laughed. "I almost didn't. When you were chasing me down the street, I almost wet myself."

"You run well. You have impressive form."

"Thanks, I think."

Her thoughts turned to poor Ella-Mae. The teenager was recovering at home. She'd dropped by this morning to see Savannah, and they'd both hugged and cried.

Ryder pressed a fresh bandage to Savannah's belly. The wound was mostly off to the side. It hurt, but the painkillers helped. The bruises on her neck were healing too, but were unfortunately turning hideous shades of green and yellow.

"How about you run away with me, Savannah?" Ryder winked again. "We can rent a yacht. Sail the Caribbean."

"Will you two quit flirting with my woman?" Hunt yelled from upstairs.

Savannah smiled. She tapped Ryder's nose. "Someday, some woman is going to knock you off-kilter. And she'll be impervious to all that Ryder Morgan charm."

"Never." His gaze flicked up to her painting. The one of her and Hunt. He'd hung it in the living room. She wasn't sure how she felt about it since she was naked in it, but she hoped she could talk him into putting it back in the bedroom eventually.

"He loves you," Ryder said.

Her heart skipped a beat. She still couldn't quite believe it. "I know."

"He'd do anything for you. Kill for you. Die for you. Give you everything you need."

She looked down at her hands.

Ryder put a finger under her chin and tipped it up. "If you let him. You guys are two peas in a pod. You take on all the responsibility for everyone and everything, then drown in your guilt when you feel you don't live up to all those expectations."

"Ryder—"

"Neither of you believe you deserve the good stuff. Let him love you, Savannah. And show him that he deserves that too, despite whatever fucked-up shit from the past, whatever shit he sees daily on the job, messes with his head."

"I love him, Ryder. So much it scares me." She felt Cam watching.

"Then I guess that's how you know it's the real deal," Ryder said.

"He's right. I do love you."

She looked up and saw Hunt on the stairs. He was wearing jeans and a T-shirt, a bandage on his arm.

Cam stood. "That's our cue to leave."

Ryder hesitated. "I was hoping to bum lunch."

"I'll buy you a burger," Cam said.

Savannah barely glanced at them as the two men left.

"I just finished speaking with my lieutenant," Hunt said.

Her pulse jerked. "Walkson?"

"Is locked up, baby. Forever." Hunt circled his hands over her shoulders.

"There'll be a trial—"

"He won't be getting off on murder. Or for attacking you and Ella-Mae, or hiring someone to shoot a cop. I've already been in contact with the other states where Killian clocked potential victims. Brynn is taking point, and my cousin misses nothing. Walkson will die in prison."

Savannah nodded. "How come you aren't taking point?"

"Because I asked my lieutenant for some time off." Hunt rubbed a thumb over her lips. "I told him that I needed to heal. And spend some time with my woman while she heals. So, I have two weeks off."

Two weeks of just her and Hunt. It sounded like heaven.

"You ready to see your mom and brother?" he asked.

Her belly clenched. "Soon." She'd talked with them on the phone. They'd been hurt and angry that she'd run, even to protect them. But they'd also been happy and relieved she was alive and okay. Her mom had cried. Ezra, who sounded so grown up now and had finished college, had been quietly furious.

"We all need a little time to adjust," she said.

Plus, she realized it was hard to go back. Things, people, feelings morphed and changed over time. You could only ever move forward.

Savannah was ready to do that. With this man right here.

He kissed her slowly and steadily. He'd been so careful with her since they'd left the hospital last night. She pulled closer to him, and tried to deepen the kiss, but he leaned back.

She growled. "I'm fine."

"You were stabbed. I'm going to make sure you're fully healed before we get naked."

Savannah looked at the ceiling. "I guess it's my fault for falling for a do-gooder, overprotective, alpha-male detective."

"At least you finally admit you fell for me."

"I did. I never stood a chance."

He pulled her close. "So, you're going to stay? Here in San Francisco? Move in here with me?"

Everything in her trembled. Just weeks ago, she'd been terrified, living on the run, unable to live a normal life.

Now, this man meant everything to her.

"I'll stay. Wherever you are, that's where I want to be."

His smile lit up his rugged face. Oh, she needed to sketch him, just like that. This time, she kissed him. When he pulled back, she was extremely gratified to find that he was hard, his cock nudging her belly.

She rubbed against him and he gripped her hip. "Tease."

She liked the growl in his voice.

"I bet we could find something non-jostling and not too strenuous to do in bed," she suggested.

He frowned.

"Please, Hunter?" she begged.

Heat flared in his eyes. "I think, if you promise to lie on your back and not move, I could think of something to do to you—" he nipped her lip "—with my hands, my mouth..."

Flames licked her insides. "I'll meet you upstairs."

As she carefully made her way up the stairs—her wound didn't let her move very fast—she loved the sound of his laughter behind her.

HUNT SAT in his chair in the park, under the dappled shade of the trees. He had his sunglasses on, and the squeal of kids playing in the nearby playground filled his ears, but his focus was on Savannah.

She stood at her easel, painting. He'd helped to set it up, while arguing with her about lifting anything.

In the four days since she'd been stabbed, she was healing well. Both inside and out.

She was blossoming, slowly coming out of the shadows of her years-long ordeal, and believing that she was free and safe.

She slept soundly in his arms every night, smiled as they shared meals, and the look on her face when he touched her body always took his breath away.

His gorgeous artist was starting to believe.

The gang had descended the night before with take-out, beer, and wine. Savannah had snort-laughed with Gia, Haven, Harlow, Maggie, and Brynn. Only Sofie and Rome had been missing, off at some charity engagement in Los Angeles.

Hunt watched Savannah frown and daub more paint on her canvas. She was in one of his old shirts, tiny black shorts underneath. His shirt was already covered in splatters of paint.

He wanted his ring on her finger, wanted to talk about looking for a house in the suburbs. One with a huge room for an art studio. A home that could be theirs.

But he knew it was still too soon. He wanted to wait until the last of the shadows that Walkson had put in her eyes were gone.

There was time. She loved him and he loved her. He'd know when the time was right.

"I can feel you staring at me," she called out.

"You're mine, and you're good to stare at, so I don't see the problem."

She shot him a smile.

"I was thinking you owe me quite a few shirts."

Her smile widened and she set her brush down. "Maybe I'll get you some nice, tie-dyed ones."

She grabbed a water bottle and sipped.

"I got a phone call earlier," he told her.

"Oh?" She raised a brow.

He didn't miss the faint tension in her. She still expected bad news. It would fade in time. "Marcie Garoppolo filed for divorce."

"Oh." Savannah dropped the water bottle and clapped her hands together. "That's great news!"

"Yeah. She didn't press charges, but she's left him and moved back in with her parents."

"I hope she gets a second chance and a happy ending." Savannah wandered over to him.

He nabbed her and tumbled her onto his lap.

"Hunter, I'm not sure this camp chair will hold us both."

"It'll hold." He nuzzled her neck, discreetly checking his watch. Cam was due to arrive soon with a surprise.

"So, I was thinking..." Her tone was cautious.

"What?"

She set her shoulders back. "I was talking with Ryder."

"Now I'm worried."

She whacked his shoulder playfully. "I'm thinking I'll get my scars removed."

Hunt stilled, his gaze on her face.

"I know they aren't that bad, and you've helped me accept them, but he put them there. They're a reminder of him, and he's not a part of my life anymore."

"Whatever you want, baby, I'll support you. Leave them, get them removed, I'll love you either way."

"I love you, Detective Morgan. Boy, am I glad that I played my music too loud."

Hunt smiled. "Me too, baby."

He pulled that delectable mouth to his. As he kissed her, the world fell away and it was just the two of them. And the bright future they had ahead of them.

His phone vibrated in his pocket. It was probably Cam telling Hunt that he was close to arriving, but when Savannah climbed around to straddle him and kissed him harder and with great enthusiasm, all he could do was hold on and groan.

"Savannah." He managed to break the kiss. "I have a surprise for you."

She waggled her eyebrows. "I know." She purposely shifted on his erection, tearing another groan from him.

Over her shoulder, he saw a X6 pull up at the park.

He looked back at her beautiful face, the wind playing with some of her curls. He clamped a hand on her hip. "That's not it, and that can't be a surprise, since you just breathing seems to make me hard."

She rubbed her nose against his. "I hope that when we're both old, and gray, and our wrinkles have wrinkles, you still have that problem."

He pinched her butt and urged her to stand. He stood and took a second to readjust himself. Hopefully he could get himself under control in the next few minutes.

He watched Cam circle the X6. He helped an older, blonde lady out of the passenger seat. The back door opened, and a tall, handsome, twenty-something man got out. The breeze tousled his dirty-blond curls. He scanned the park. A woman Savannah's age exited last—tall, slender, with inky-black hair. She nudged the young man, searching the park as well.

Hunt turned to Savannah. "Here's your surprise."

Frowning, she turned, and took a second. Then she noticed the trio. Her body went stiff as a board. "Oh, my God."

He slid a comforting hand down her arm. "I know you've talked with them, but they wanted to see you. And I think you needed to see them."

She swallowed and looked up at him, her pretty, gray eyes shining.

"Go," he urged her.

She walked toward the approaching group, then she was running.

Savannah and her mother collided first. Savannah was laughing and crying. Her mother kept touching Savannah like she was reassuring herself that her daughter was real.

Ezra claimed Savannah next. The young man wasn't crying, but his face was filled with emotion.

Then Saskia Hawke leaped on Savannah. The women hugged, cried, and laughed. The sound of their happy laughter rang through the park.

Camden reached Hunt, his eyes hidden behind his sunglasses. "Nice work, bro."

Hunt lifted his chin. "She needed it. Needed to reconnect with them. She was just afraid to close the gap."

Cam nodded. "The gap can feel like a chasm sometimes."

Hunt looked at his brother.

"I'm fine. My chasm lasted about an hour. You, Ryder, and Mom just leaped across it when I got back. It didn't feel like that for long. So, thanks for being there."

Hunt clasped Cam's shoulder. "We're always here for you."

Savannah, holding her mom's hand, led the group over.

"You've met Camden, but I really want you to meet my detective." She smiled at Hunt.

Mrs. Hart met his gaze and nodded. "Thank you, Detective Morgan. For bringing her back to us and making her safe."

"It's Hunt." He slung an arm around Savannah's shoulders, and she leaned into him.

Mrs. Hart watched them, her eyes filling with happy tears.

Ezra nodded and shook Hunt's hand. Hunt shook Saskia's slim hand last.

"Your brother was a big help," Hunt told her.

"He always is." Saskia smiled. "He has his finger on the pulse of, well, everything." She looked at Savannah. "Nice." She tilted her head toward Hunt. "The men here in San Francisco..." Saskia fanned herself.

Savannah smiled. "There are more of them, but most of them are taken." Savannah shot a sly look at Camden. "Except for Hunt's brothers."

Cam dragged in a breath and looked resigned.

Savannah laughed. "I've missed years of teasing my brother, so I have lots to catch up on."

Ezra and Cam shared a look.

As Savannah laughed again, sounding carefree and happy, Hunt pressed a kiss to her temple.

All was right in his pocket of the world.

CHAPTER TWENTY

"Oh, boy."

Savannah brushed past Hunt, grabbed his glass of Blanton Gold, and chugged it.

"Easy, baby." He stroked her back, trying to ease her nerves. He enjoyed that her sexy, red cocktail dress left most of her back bare.

She huffed out a breath.

"Just relax," he said.

"You relax." She dragged in a breath. "Sorry, I'm just really, really nervous."

He cupped her cheek, careful not to wreck her makeup. "It's your first art showing in years. You're entitled to some nerves." He lowered his voice. "Have I told you how much I like your dress?"

Her gray gaze met his and she smiled. "No, but you gave it away when I set it out on the bed and you took one look, then dragged me down on the floor and made love to me."

He smiled. "I like the dress, and I like the way you wear it even more."

She touched her silky hair. Over the last few weeks, she'd let it return to her more natural silvery blonde. Right now, it was up in a sleek roll.

She snagged a flute of champagne from a passing server and sipped. "There are so many people."

There were. They were in a wing of the Hutton Museum. Over the last few weeks, Haven had worked her butt off, pulling the showing together. Savannah had worked her butt off, too, creating new paintings and sculptures for the show. Haven had also had several of Savannah's sketches framed and displayed.

Thankfully, none were of him naked.

He'd turned his guest room on the top floor beside his master bedroom into an art studio for her. She loved it. She spent hours in there, her music pumping. She'd also hired Ella-Mae, who did jobs for Savannah—replenishing art supplies, packing up artwork, helping to keep the studio clean.

The teenager had fully recovered from her ordeal. Her parents had gotten her to see a therapist, and that had helped him convince Savannah to talk to someone, too.

Each day, she was lighter. Trusting her new life more and more, and leaving Andrew Walkson behind. The man had been sentenced, and was up on new charges for the additional women he'd murdered in Kansas, Colorado, and Florida. He would never see the light of day as a free man.

"God, you look so handsome in your tux." Savannah fiddled with his bowtie.

"The showing's going to be great. People are already loving your art." He turned her. "Look."

There were lots of people, all dressed in tuxedos and fancy dresses. Haven was talking with an elegant-looking couple who were staring intently at one of Savannah's paintings.

"It doesn't feel real," Savannah murmured. "It's like a dream."

"It's real." He slid a hand down to her stomach. She'd had the work done on the scars. There would always be something there, but they were hardly noticeable now.

She didn't seem to think about them anymore.

"I lost everything, now I have everything and more." She spun. "I'm really, really glad my grumpy, detective neighbor came thumping on my door."

"Me too, baby." He kissed her. "Love you."

"I love you too, Hunter."

"Excuse me." Haven appeared in a long, pretty, purple dress, sounding bossy. "You don't get to monopolize the woman of the night, Hunt." Haven took Savannah's arm. "Come on. There are lots of people who want to meet the artist, and spend lots of money."

As Haven pulled her away, Savannah shot him a look that was part terrified, part excited.

He smiled and sipped his bourbon.

"Looks like Savannah's showing is a big success." Vander stepped up beside him.

Vander somehow managed to look dark and dangerous in his tuxedo. He cradled a glass of something amber. Probably a hell of a lot more expensive than Hunt's Blanton.

"Lots of sold stickers already," Easton said, from the other side of Vander. The billionaire looked like he wore a tux every day.

"I'm damn proud of her," Hunt said. "She deserves this."

He planned to give her everything she deserved. All the things that had been denied to her for so long.

"I might have purchased that sculpture called *Woman* for an exorbitant amount," Easton said. "I'm pretty sure Haven hosed me."

Hunt had admired the piece and been lucky enough to see it being created. It was a woman with her arms raised above her head, her naked body covered in a tiny wisp of fabric. Savannah had worked on it for days. It was both elegant and sensuous.

Hunt's lips quirked. "I take it you recognize the model."

Easton's eyes flashed. "I recognize my woman's naked body when I see it."

Vander grinned.

"Brynn posed for Savannah as well," Hunt said. "The piece isn't finished yet."

"Shit." Vander's smile disappeared. "I'll buy it before it goes to a showing."

Hunt heard music start up in the back corner. There was a small band, and later there'd be a jazz singer and dancing. He planned to lure his woman onto the dance floor, and have her in his arms, as soon as she was finished hobnobbing.

She deserved to bask in her success.

He watched her talk with a trio of potential buyers. She gestured to the painting on the wall, then she glanced over and saw him watching her.

She blew him a kiss.

"Careful," Vander warned. "You keep looking at her like that, and the place will go up in flames."

"I get how you feel now, Vander. About Brynn."

Vander's gaze shifted, zeroing in on Brynn. Hunt's cousin wore a sexy, one-shouldered dress in a pretty blue-gray. She was laughing with Harlow and Gia.

"You'd take on the world for them," Vander murmured. "Stop anything from hurting them, all so they'll look at you with love on their face."

Hunt nodded. "Exactly like that." He held his glass up. "Here's to the love of a good woman."

Vander touched his glass to Hunt's.

Ryder and Camden appeared.

"What are we toasting?" Ryder asked.

"Loving a good woman," Hunt told him.

Ryder shook his head. "I like to spread the joy. The 'one woman' thing isn't for me."

Easton, Vander, and Hunt all traded a look.

Cam stayed silent, but as Hunt followed his brother's gaze, he saw him looking at Saskia Hawke. Savannah's best friend had flown in for the showing. She was slim, with a body suited to the ballerina she was. She looked stunning in a black sheath dress.

"Your time will come," Easton told Ryder.

"Nope." Ryder sipped his beer, then half choked. "Who is *that*?"

Hunt turned. A woman stalked along the edge of the dance floor wearing a shimmery, metallic dress in blood-red. It clung to her long, fit body, molding over an ass that deserved more than a second look. It had tiny, spaghetti straps, and no back. It dipped all the way down to the top of her spectacular ass. Her long, brown hair—streaked with gold—was loose.

Vander made a sound. "That's the newest Norcross Security employee. Siv Pedersen."

"Seeve," Ryder repeated. "I wonder if she likes to dance."

"Careful," Vander warned. "She's ex-Norwegian special forces, with a specialty in Arctic warfare and oil rig security."

"Sounds badass," Hunt said.

Ryder set his drink down and straightened his bowtie. "I'll be back."

Hunt shook his head. His brother had always liked a challenge...and getting himself into trouble.

Once again, Hunt scanned the room and found Savannah. Yes, when the right one appeared, it made everything worthwhile.

Eric, Mitchell, and Manny hadn't made it home. They'd died for their country, but Hunt would live—in their memory, for Savannah, and for himself.

OKAY, she was giddy.

And it wasn't just from the copious amounts of very excellent champagne.

"I hope you can't die from happiness," Savannah said.

"Nope," Haven replied. "I can confirm that." The woman's smile sparkled. "You're a huge success, Savannah Cole."

"I am." There were so many sold stickers. People had loved the showing and her artwork. "All thanks to you."

Haven shook her head. "No, thanks to your talent."

"My art is being appreciated, I'm safe, and I'm in love with a hot detective."

Hunter was in a huddle of handsome hotness with some of the Norcross men.

"You totally deserve it all." Gia held up a bottle of Moët and topped up Savannah's glass. "And I bought two pieces for myself. Saxon got a third."

"That nude of the curvy brunette." Haven winked.

"You can't tell it's me," Gia said. "My face is obscured."

"He could," Haven said.

Savannah sipped, enjoying the bubbles on her lips. "Just weeks ago, I had nothing. And now..." She saw her mom and brother dancing together. They were laughing. Her mom called Savannah every other day, and Savannah and Hunt were planning a trip to New York in the near future. Her mom still tripped up occasionally and called her Susannah, but it was less often now. They were still working through some of the pain and hurt, but love shone through strongly.

And her mom loved Hunt.

Savannah scanned the room and spotted Camden, lurking in the shadows on the edge of the room. As she watched, a pretty blonde approached him. The woman said something, smiled hopefully, and waved at the dance floor.

Cam shook his head.

The blonde wrinkled her nose, then slipped away. *Hmm.* Savannah would have to work on the man she considered an honorary brother. Cam deserved someone special. Someone who made him happy.

Then she saw Cam straighten, staring intently.

Who was he staring at? Savannah craned her neck, trying to get a better look. He pushed off the wall and stalked across the room. That's when Savannah saw that he was following Saskia into the next room.

Savannah's mouth dropped open. She might be reading too much into it... But the more she thought about it, the more she decided her confident, beautiful friend would be *perfect* for Cam.

If she didn't live on the other side of the country.

Hmm, well, any obstacle could be surmounted.

"Can I dance with the wildly successful artist?"

Hunt's deep voice pulled her away from her musings, and she spun. "Yes, you can."

Her man led her to the dance floor and twirled her into his arms. She breathed in his scent—Hunt's sandalwood cologne permeated with his own scent.

"I'm so proud of you," he murmured.

She flushed. "Thank you. I wouldn't be here without you."

"We make an excellent team."

Gia and Saxon danced passed them. The pair moved well together.

"And I love your brothers and your friends," Savannah added.

"They love you back."

"You're a cocky, arrogant ass," a sharp female voice snapped.

They swiveled and saw Ryder on the dance floor, facing off with a stunning woman in a metallic, red dress.

"Uh-oh," Hunt muttered.

The woman wasn't pretty, exactly, but she was striking. Her brown hair was shot through with streaks of gold, and her face was all slim, sharp features. Her arms were very toned and she looked fit.

"Babe, I'm just confident," Ryder said

The woman rolled her eyes and crossed her arms over her chest.

"Wow, a woman who's not impressed with Ryder's charm," Savannah murmured.

Hunt grunted.

Ryder smiled and said something else to the woman, too low for Savannah to hear.

Then she didn't see exactly what the woman did, but her leg moved and hooked Ryder's ankle. He went down hard, flat on his back, in the middle of the dance floor.

The woman smiled, then turned, and stalked off, her red dress swishing behind her.

"Wow, she's awesome," Savannah breathed.

Ryder sat up, staring hungrily after the woman.

Hunt shook his head. "It's lucky my brother has a hard head." Hunt pulled Savannah closer. "Enough of my brother. I want to know when we can sneak out of here and go home?" He nipped her jaw. "I really, really want to peel you out of this dress."

Desire flickered in her belly. "Why, Detective Morgan..."

His gaze traced over her face. "Every smile, every laugh, every time you look at me with love in your eyes, I feel like the luckiest man in the world."

She melted. "Oh, Hunter." They kissed, right there in the middle of the dance floor. "Let's go now."

"You sure?"

She nodded, hungry for him. "If I get into trouble with Haven, I'll tell her it was your fault."

Hunt laughed. "I don't know, Haven's meaner than she looks."

"I'll have to give you some incentive." Savannah went on her toes and whispered exactly what she planned to do to him once they got home.

"Fuck." He squeezed her hand and dragged her off the dance floor.

Savannah laughed. "I have to say goodbye—"

"You'll see everyone tomorrow." He pulled her close. "You're mine now, Savannah Cole."

Her chest filled with warmth. She felt so light, happy, free.

"I sure am. Now take me home, Detective."

I hope you enjoyed Hunt and Savannah's story!

Norcross Security continues with *The Medic*,

starring the next Morgan brother, Ryder, and the tough, new female recruit at Norcross Security. *The Medic* releases on the 5th of April.

For more action romance (and some more cameos by Killian Hawke and Vander Norcross), check out the first book in the **Billionaire Heists trilogy**, *Stealing from Mr. Rich* (Zane Roth's story). **Read on for a preview of the first chapter.**

Don't miss out! For updates about new releases, free books, and other fun stuff, sign up for my VIP mailing list and get your *free box set* containing three action-packed romances.

Visit here to get started: www.annahackett.com

Would you like a FREE BOX SET of my books?

PREVIEW: STEALING FROM MR. RICH

Monroe

The old-fashioned Rosengrens safe was a beauty.

I carefully turned the combination dial, then pressed closer to the safe. The metal was cool under my fingertips. The safe wasn't pretty, but stout and secure. There was something to be said for solid security.

Rosengrens had started making safes in Sweden over a hundred years ago. They were good at it. I listened to the pins, waiting for contact. Newer safes had internals made from lightweight materials to reduce sensory feedback, so I didn't get to use these skills very often.

Some people could play the piano, I could play a safe. The tiny vibration I was waiting for reached my fingertips, followed by the faintest click.

"I've gotcha, old girl." The Rosengrens had quite a few quirks, but my blood sang as I moved the dial again.

I heard a louder click and spun the handle.

The safe door swung open. Inside, I saw stacks of jewelry cases and wads of hundred-dollar bills. *Nice.*

Standing, I dusted my hands off on my jeans. "There you go, Mr. Goldstein."

"You are a doll, Monroe O'Connor. Thank you."

The older man, dressed neatly in pressed chinos and a blue shirt, grinned at me. He had coke-bottle glasses, wispy, white hair, and a wrinkled face.

I smiled at him. Mr. Goldstein was one of my favorite people. "I'll send you my bill."

His grin widened. "I don't know what I'd do without you."

I raised a brow. "You could stop forgetting your safe combination."

The wealthy old man called me every month or so to open his safe. Right now, we were standing in the home office of his expensive Park Avenue penthouse.

It was decorated in what I thought of as "rich, old man." There were heavy drapes, gold-framed artwork, lots of dark wood—including the built-in shelves around the safe—and a huge desk.

"Then I wouldn't get to see your pretty face," he said.

I smiled and patted his shoulder. "I'll see you next month, Mr. Goldstein." The poor man was lonely. His wife had died the year before, and his only son lived in Europe.

"Sure thing, Monroe. I'll have some of those donuts you like."

We headed for the front door and my chest tightened. I understood feeling lonely. "You could do with some new locks on your door. I mean, your building has top-notch security, but you can never be too careful. Pop by the shop if you want to talk locks."

He beamed at me and held the door open. "I might do that."

"Bye, Mr. Goldstein."

I headed down the plush hall to the elevator. Everything in the building screamed old money. I felt like an imposter just being in the building. Like I had "daughter of a criminal" stamped on my head.

Pulling out my cell phone, I pulled up my accounting app and entered Mr. Goldstein's callout. Next, I checked my messages.

Still nothing from Maguire.

Frowning, I bit my lip. That made it three days since I'd heard from my little brother. I shot him off a quick text.

"Text me back, Mag," I muttered.

The elevator opened and I stepped in, trying not to

worry about Maguire. He was an adult, but I'd practically raised him. Most days it felt like I had a twenty-four-year-old kid.

The elevator slowed and stopped at another floor. An older, well-dressed couple entered. They eyed me and my well-worn jeans like I'd crawled out from under a rock.

I smiled. "Good morning."

Yeah, yeah, I'm not wearing designer duds, and my bank account doesn't have a gazillion zeros. You're so much better than me.

Ignoring them, I scrolled through Instagram. When we finally reached the lobby, the couple shot me another dubious look before they left. I strode out across the marble-lined space and rolled my eyes.

During my teens, I'd cared about what people thought. Everyone had known that my father was Terry O'Connor—expert thief, safecracker, and con man. I'd felt every repulsed look and sly smirk at high school.

Then I'd grown up, cultivated some thicker skin, and learned not to care. *Fuck 'em.* People who looked down on others for things outside their control were assholes.

I wrinkled my nose. Okay, it was easier said than done.

When I walked outside, the street was busy. I smiled, breathing in the scent of New York—car exhaust, burnt meat, and rotting trash. Besides, most people cared more about themselves. They judged you, left you bleeding, then forgot you in the blink of an eye.

I unlocked my bicycle, and pulled on my helmet, then set off down the street. I needed to get to the store.

The ride wasn't long, but I spent every second worrying about Mag.

My brother had a knack for finding trouble. I sighed. After a childhood, where both our mothers had taken off, and Da was in and out of jail, Mag was entitled to being a bit messed up. The O'Connors were a long way from the Brady Bunch.

I pulled up in front of my shop in Hell's Kitchen and stopped for a second.

I grinned. *All mine.*

Okay, I didn't own the building, but I owned the store. The sign above the shop said *Lady Locksmith*. The logo was lipstick red—a woman's hand with gorgeous red nails, holding a set of keys.

After I locked up my bike, I strode inside. A chime sounded.

God, I loved the place. It was filled with glossy, warm-wood shelves lined with displays of state-of-the-art locks and safes. A key-cutting machine sat at the back.

A blonde head popped up from behind a long, shiny counter.

"You're back," Sabrina said.

My best friend looked like a doll—small, petite, with a head of golden curls.

We'd met doing our business degrees at college, and had become fast friends. Sabrina had always wanted to be tall and sexy, but had to settle for small and cute. She was my manager, and was getting married in a month.

"Yeah, Mr. Goldstein forgot his safe code again," I said.

Sabrina snorted. "That old coot doesn't forget, he just likes looking at your ass."

"He's harmless. He's nice, and lonely. How's the team doing?"

Sabrina leaned forward, pulling out her tablet. I often wondered if she slept with it. "Liz is out back unpacking stock." Sabrina's nose wrinkled. "McRoberts overcharged us on the Schlage locks again."

"That prick." He was always trying to screw me over. "I'll call him."

"Paola, Kat, and Isabella are all out on jobs."

Excellent. Business was doing well. Lady Locksmith specialized in providing female locksmiths to all the single ladies of New York. They also advised on how to keep them safe—securing locks, doors, and windows.

I had a dream of one day seeing multiple Lady Locksmiths around the city. Hell, around every city. A girl could dream. Growing up, once I understood the damage my father did to other people, all I'd wanted was to be respectable. To earn my own way and add to the world, not take from it.

"Did you get that new article I sent you to post on the blog?" I asked.

Sabrina nodded. "It'll go live shortly, and then I'll post on Insta, as well."

When I had the time, I wrote articles on how women —single *and* married—should secure their homes. My latest was aimed at domestic-violence survivors, and helping them feel safe. I donated my time to Nightingale House, a local shelter that helped women leaving DV situations, and I installed locks for them, free of charge.

"We should start a podcast," Sabrina said.

I wrinkled my nose. "I don't have time to sit around recording stuff." I did my fair share of callouts for jobs, plus at night I had to stay on top of the business-side of the store.

"Fine, fine." Sabrina leaned against the counter and eyed my jeans. "Damn, I hate you for being tall, long, and gorgeous. You're going to look *way* too beautiful as my maid of honor." She waved a hand between us. "You're all tall, sleek, and dark-haired, and I'm...the opposite."

I had some distant Black Irish ancestor to thank for my pale skin and ink-black hair. Growing up, I wanted to be short, blonde, and tanned. I snorted. "Beauty comes in all different forms, Sabrina." I gripped her shoulders. "You are so damn pretty, and your fiancé happens to think you are the most beautiful woman in the world. Andrew is gaga over you."

Sabrina sighed happily. "He does and he is." A pause. "So, do you have a date for my wedding yet?" My bestie's voice turned breezy and casual.

Uh-oh. I froze. All the wedding prep had sent my normally easygoing best friend a bit crazy. And I knew very well not to trust that tone.

I edged toward my office. "Not yet."

Sabrina's blue eyes sparked. "It's only *four* weeks away, Monroe. The maid of honor can't come alone."

"I'll be busy helping you out—"

"Find a date, Monroe."

"I don't want to just pick anyone for your wedding—"

Sabrina stomped her foot. "Find someone, or I'll find someone for you."

I held up my hands. "Okay, okay." I headed for my office. "I'll—" My cell phone rang. *Yes.* "I've got a call. Got to go." I dove through the office door.

"I won't forget," Sabrina yelled. "I'll revoke your best-friend status, if I have to."

I closed the door on my bridezilla bestie and looked at the phone.

Maguire. Finally.

I stabbed the call button. "Where have you been?"

"We have your brother," a robotic voice said.

My blood ran cold. My chest felt like it had filled with concrete.

"If you want to keep him alive, you'll do exactly as I say."

Zane

God, this party was boring.

Zane Roth sipped his wine and glanced around the ballroom at the Mandarin Oriental. The party held the Who's Who of New York society, all dressed up in their glittering best. The ceiling shimmered with a sea of crystal lights, tall flower arrangements dominated the tables, and the wall of windows had a great view of the Manhattan skyline.

Everything was picture perfect...and boring.

If it wasn't for the charity auction, he wouldn't be dressed in his tuxedo and dodging annoying people.

"I'm so sick of these parties," he muttered.

A snort came from beside him.

One of his best friends, Maverick Rivera, sipped his wine. "You were voted New York's sexiest billionaire bachelor. You should be loving this shindig."

Mav had been one of his best friends since college. Like Zane, Maverick hadn't come from wealth. They'd both earned it the old-fashioned way. Zane loved numbers and money, and had made Wall Street his hunting ground. Mav was a geek, despite not looking like a stereotypical one. He'd grown up in a strong, Mexican-American family, and with his brown skin, broad shoulders, and the fact that he worked out a lot, no one would pick him for a tech billionaire.

But under the big body, the man was a computer geek to the bone.

"All the society mamas are giving you lots of speculative looks." Mav gave him a small grin.

"Shut it, Rivera."

"They're all dreaming of marrying their daughters off to billionaire Zane Roth, the finance King of Wall Street."

Zane glared. "You done?"

"Oh, I could go on."

"I seem to recall another article about the billionaire bachelors. All three of us." Zane tipped his glass at his friend. "They'll be coming for you, next."

Mav's smile dissolved, and he shrugged a broad shoulder. "I'll toss Kensington at them. He's pretty."

Liam Kensington was the third member of their trio.

Unlike Zane and Mav, Liam had come from money, although he worked hard to avoid his bloodsucking family.

Zane saw a woman in a slinky, blue dress shoot him a welcoming smile.

He looked away.

When he'd made his first billion, he'd welcomed the attention. Especially the female attention. He'd bedded more than his fair share of gorgeous women.

Of late, nothing and no one caught his interest. Women all left him feeling numb.

Work. He thrived on that.

A part of him figured he'd never find a woman who made him feel the same way as his work.

"Speak of the devil," Mav said.

Zane looked up to see Liam Kensington striding toward them. With the lean body of a swimmer, clad in a perfectly tailored tuxedo, he looked every inch the billionaire. His gold hair complemented a face the ladies oohed over.

People tried to get his attention, but the real estate mogul ignored everyone.

He reached Zane and Mav, grabbed Zane's wine, and emptied it in two gulps.

"I hate this party. When can we leave?" Having spent his formative years in London, he had a posh British accent. Another thing the ladies loved. "I have a contract to work on, my fundraiser ball to plan, and things to catch up on after our trip to San Francisco."

The three of them had just returned from a business trip to the West Coast.

"Can't leave until the auction's done," Zane said.

Liam sighed. His handsome face often had him voted the best-looking billionaire bachelor.

"Buy up big," Zane said. "Proceeds go to the Boys and Girls Clubs."

"One of your pet charities," Liam said.

"Yeah." Zane's father had left when he was seven. His mom had worked hard to support them. She was his hero. He liked to give back to charities that supported kids growing up in tough circumstances.

He'd set his mom up in a gorgeous house Upstate that she loved. And he was here for her tonight.

"Don't bid on the Phillips-Morley necklace, though," he added. "It's mine."

The necklace had a huge, rectangular sapphire pendant surrounded by diamonds. It was the real-life necklace said to have inspired the necklace in the movie, *Titanic*. It had been given to a young woman, Kate Florence Phillips, by her lover, Henry Samuel Morley. The two had run away together and booked passage on the Titanic.

Unfortunately for poor Kate, Henry had drowned when the ship had sunk. She'd returned to England with the necklace and a baby in her belly.

Zane's mother had always loved the story and pored over pictures of the necklace. She'd told him the story of the lovers, over and over.

"It was a gift from a man to a woman he loved. She was a shop girl, and he owned the store, but they fell in love, even though society frowned on their love." She sighed. "That's true love, Zane. Devotion, loyalty, through the good times and the bad."

Everything Carol Roth had never known.

Of course, it turned out old Henry was much older than his lover, and already married. But Zane didn't want to ruin the fairy tale for his mom.

Now, the Phillips-Morley necklace had turned up, and was being offered at auction. And Zane was going to get it for his mom. It was her birthday in a few months.

"Hey, is your fancy, new safe ready yet?" Zane asked Mav.

His friend nodded. "You're getting one of the first ones. I can have my team install it this week."

"Perfect." Mav's new Riv3000 was the latest in high-tech safes and said to be unbreakable. "I'll keep the necklace in it until my mom's birthday."

Someone called out Liam's name. With a sigh, their friend forced a smile. "Can't dodge this one. Simpson's an investor in my Brooklyn project. I'll be back."

"Need a refill?" Zane asked Mav.

"Sure."

Zane headed for the bar. He'd almost reached it when a manicured hand snagged his arm.

"Zane."

He looked down at the woman and barely swallowed his groan. "Allegra. You look lovely this evening."

She did. Allegra Montgomery's shimmery, silver dress hugged her slender figure, and her cloud of mahogany brown hair accented her beautiful face. As the only daughter of a wealthy New York family—her father was from *the* Montgomery family and her mother was a former Miss America—Allegra was well-bred and well-educated but also, as he'd discovered, spoiled and liked getting her way.

Her dark eyes bored into him. "I'm sorry things ended badly for us the other month. I was..." Her voice lowered, and she stroked his forearm. "I miss you. I was hoping we could catch up again."

Zane arched a brow. They'd dated for a few weeks, shared a few dinners, and some decent sex. But Allegra liked being the center of attention, complained that he worked too much, and had constantly hounded him to take her on vacation. Preferably on a private jet to Tahiti or the Maldives.

When she'd asked him if it would be too much for him to give her a credit card of her own, for monthly expenses, Zane had exited stage left.

"I don't think so, Allegra. We aren't...compatible."

Her full lips turned into a pout. "I thought we were *very* compatible."

He cleared his throat. "I heard you moved on. With Chip Huffington."

Allegra waved a hand. "Oh, that's nothing serious."

And Chip was only a millionaire. Allegra would see that as a step down. In fact, Zane felt like every time she looked at him, he could almost see little dollar signs in her eyes.

He dredged up a smile. "I wish you all the best, Allegra. Good evening." He sidestepped her and made a beeline for the bar.

"What can I get you?" the bartender asked.

Wine wasn't going to cut it. It would probably be frowned on to ask for an entire bottle of Scotch. "Two glasses of Scotch, please. On the rocks. Do you have Macallan?"

"No, sorry, sir. Will Glenfiddich do?"

"Sure."

"Ladies and gentlemen," a voice said over the loudspeaker. The lights lowered. "I hope you're ready to spend big for a wonderful cause."

Carrying the drinks, Zane hurried back to Mav and Liam. He handed Mav a glass.

"Let's do this," Mav grumbled. "And next time, I'll make a generous online donation so I don't have to come to the party."

"Drinks at my place after I get the necklace," Zane said. "I have a very good bottle of Macallan."

Mav stilled. "How good?"

"Macallan 25. Single malt."

"I'm there," Liam said.

Mav lifted his chin.

Ahead, Zane watched the evening's host lift a black cloth off a pedestal. He stared at the necklace, the sapphire glittering under the lights.

There it was.

The sapphire was a deep, rich blue. Just like all the photos his mother had shown him.

"Get that damn necklace, Roth, and let's get out of here," Mav said.

Zane nodded. He'd get the necklace for the one woman in his life who rarely asked for anything, then escape the rest of the bloodsuckers and hang with his friends.

Billionaire Heists

Stealing from Mr. Rich
Blackmailing Mr. Bossman
Hacking Mr. CEO

PREVIEW: TEAM 52 AND THS

Want to learn more about the mysterious, covert *Team 52*? Check out the first book in the series, *Mission: Her Protection.*

When Rowan's Arctic research team pulls a strange object out of the ice in Northern

Canada, things start to go wrong...very, very wrong. Rescued by a covert, black ops team, she finds herself in the powerful arms of a man with scary gold eyes. A man who vows to do everything and anything to protect her...

Dr. Rowan Schafer has learned it's best to do things herself and not depend on anyone else. Her cold, academic parents taught her that lesson. She loves the challenge of running a research base, until the day her scientists discover the object in a retreating glacier. Under attack, Rowan finds herself fighting to survive... until the mysterious Team 52 arrives.

Former special forces Marine Lachlan Hunter's military career ended in blood and screams, until he was recruited to lead a special team. A team tasked with a top-secret mission—to secure and safeguard pieces of powerful ancient technology. Married to his job, he's done too much and seen too much to risk inflicting his demons on a woman. But when his team arrives in the Arctic, he uncovers both an unexplained artifact, and a young girl from his past, now all grown up. A woman who ignites emotions inside him like never before.

But as Team 52 heads back to their base in Nevada, other hostile forces are after the artifact. Rowan finds herself under attack, and as the bullets fly, Lachlan vows to protect her at all costs. But in the face of danger like they've never seen before, will it be enough to keep her alive.

Team 52

Mission: Her Protection
Mission: Her Rescue
Mission: Her Security
Mission: Her Defense
Mission: Her Safety
Mission: Her Freedom
Mission: Her Shield
Also Available as Audiobooks!

Want to learn more about *Treasure Hunter Security*? Check out the first book in the series, *Undiscovered*, Declan Ward's action-packed story.

One former Navy SEAL. One dedicated archeologist. One secret map to a fabulous lost oasis.

Finding undiscovered treasures is always daring, dangerous, and deadly. Perfect for the men of Treasure Hunter Security. Former Navy SEAL Declan Ward is haunted by the demons of his past and throws everything he has into his security business—Treasure Hunter Security. Dangerous archeological digs – no problem. Daring expeditions – sure thing. Museum security for invaluable exhibits – easy. But on a simple dig in the Egyptian desert, he collides with a stubborn, smart archeologist, Dr. Layne Rush, and together they get swept into a deadly treasure hunt for a mythical lost oasis. When an evil from his past reappears, Declan vows to do anything to protect Layne.

Dr. Layne Rush is dedicated to building a successful career—a promise to the parents she lost far too young. But when her dig is plagued by strange accidents, targeted by a lethal black market antiquities ring, and artifacts are stolen, she is forced to turn to Treasure Hunter Security, and to the tough, sexy, and too-used-to-giving-orders Declan. Soon her organized dig morphs into a wild treasure hunt across the desert dunes.

Danger is hunting them every step of the way, and Layne and Declan must find a way to work together...to not only find the treasure but to survive.

Treasure Hunter Security

Undiscovered

Uncharted

Unexplored

Unfathomed

Untraveled
Unmapped
Unidentified
Undetected
Also Available as Audiobooks!

ALSO BY ANNA HACKETT

Norcross Security

The Investigator

The Troubleshooter

The Specialist

The Bodyguard

The Hacker

The Powerbroker

Billionaire Heists

Stealing from Mr. Rich

Blackmailing Mr. Bossman

Hacking Mr. CEO

Team 52

Mission: Her Protection

Mission: Her Rescue

Mission: Her Security

Mission: Her Defense

Mission: Her Safety

Mission: Her Freedom

Mission: Her Shield

Mission: Her Justice

Also Available as Audiobooks!

Treasure Hunter Security

Undiscovered

Uncharted

Unexplored

Unfathomed

Untraveled

Unmapped

Unidentified

Undetected

Also Available as Audiobooks!

Galactic Kings

Overlord

Emperor

Eon Warriors

Edge of Eon

Touch of Eon

Heart of Eon

Kiss of Eon

Mark of Eon

Claim of Eon

Storm of Eon

Soul of Eon

King of Eon

Also Available as Audiobooks!

Galactic Gladiators: House of Rone

Sentinel

Defender

Centurion

Paladin

Guard

Weapons Master

Also Available as Audiobooks!

Galactic Gladiators

Gladiator

Warrior

Hero

Protector

Champion

Barbarian

Beast

Rogue

Guardian

Cyborg

Imperator

Hunter

Also Available as Audiobooks!

Hell Squad

Marcus

Cruz

Gabe

Reed

Roth

Noah

Shaw

Holmes

Niko

Finn

Devlin

Theron

Hemi

Ash

Levi

Manu

Griff

Dom

Survivors

Tane

Also Available as Audiobooks!

The Anomaly Series

Time Thief

Mind Raider

Soul Stealer

Salvation

Anomaly Series Box Set

The Phoenix Adventures

Among Galactic Ruins

At Star's End

In the Devil's Nebula

On a Rogue Planet

Beneath a Trojan Moon

Beyond Galaxy's Edge

On a Cyborg Planet

Return to Dark Earth

On a Barbarian World

Lost in Barbarian Space

Through Uncharted Space

Crashed on an Ice World

Perma Series

Winter Fusion

A Galactic Holiday

Warriors of the Wind

Tempest

Storm & Seduction

Fury & Darkness

Standalone Titles

Savage Dragon

Hunter's Surrender

One Night with the Wolf

For more information visit www.annahackett.com

ABOUT THE AUTHOR

I'm a USA Today bestselling romance author who's passionate about ***fast-paced, emotion-filled*** contemporary romantic suspense and science fiction romance. I love writing about people overcoming unbeatable odds and achieving seemingly impossible goals. I like to believe it's possible for all of us to do the same.

I live in Australia with my own personal hero and two very busy, always-on-the-move sons.

For release dates, behind-the-scenes info, free books, and other fun stuff, sign up for the latest news here:

Website: www.annahackett.com

Made in the USA
Las Vegas, NV
13 July 2024

92265298R00154